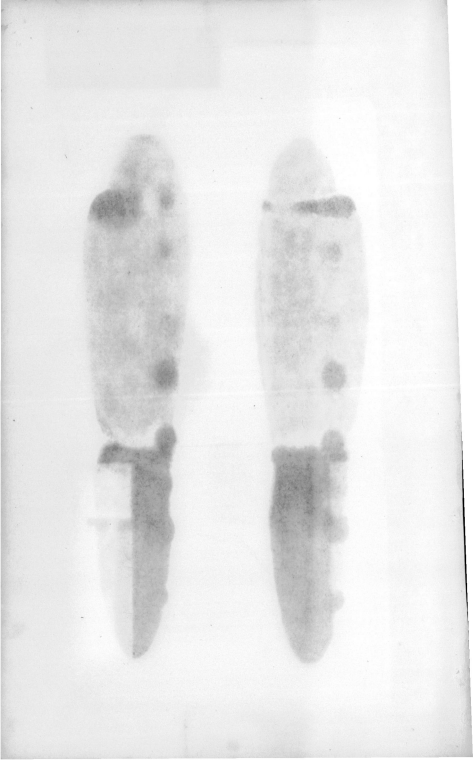

WHY MURDER?

WHY MURDER?

Judson Philips

A RED BADGE NOVEL OF SUSPENSE

DODD, MEAD & COMPANY
NEW YORK

1 2 3 4 5 6 7 8 9 10

Library of Congress Cataloging in Publication Data

Philips, Judson Pentecost, date
    Why murder?

    I. Title.
PZ3.P5412Wk [PS3531.H442]   813'.5'2   79-1066
ISBN   0-396-07683-1

PART ONE

1

Most people who read or hear about murder and violence reassure themselves with the thought that nothing like that happens to people they know. The victims and the villains belong in another world, another city, another part of town. They tell themselves it can't happen to them or to their friends.

Then, one day, it does happen.

When a man like Robert Dale is murdered, a popular movie star, a visitor in millions of American homes by way of their television screens, people realize it can happen to someone they know—even though they didn't really know Bob Dale. He was a friend they had never actually met, a lover with whom they had never actually made love. The sense of personal loss was real. The shock created by the viciousness of his killing was real. People in millions of homes grieved for him and demanded the capture of his murderer and the sternest kind of justice.

Peter Styles, investigative reporter for *Newsview Magazine*, didn't get the news of Robert Dale's murder through the ordinary channels. He was taking what might have been called a sabbatical summer from his job, trying to finish a book he was writing about terrorists and their activities all over the world. It was a subject of which he had a bitter and very personal knowledge. A year and a half before, his wife, Grace, had been the victim of senseless massacre by a terrorist group.

Styles had rented a cottage in the Berkshires and shut himself off from his friends and associates, determined to finish what he had been working at piecemeal ever since Grace's death. He had to be done with the book to get it out of his system, to try to live a life again with the tragedy behind him.

When the phone rang that morning, just as he was rolling a blank sheet of paper into his typewriter, he sat frowning, listening to the persistent ringing. He had arranged for an unlisted number. Only one person had it—Frank Devery, publisher and editor of *Newsview* and his closest friend. Devery wouldn't call him unless it was an emergency. Probably someone had accidentally dialed a wrong number.

Styles let it ring itself out, but then, immediately, it started again. He swore softly under his breath and crossed the room to the phone.

"Yes?" he said.

"Peter?" It wasn't Devery. The voice was familiar but for just a moment he couldn't place it. "Greg Maxvil here."

Lieutenant Gregory Maxvil of Manhattan's Homicide Squad was another old friend. He must have gotten the number from Devery.

"You heard the news?" Maxvil asked when Peter didn't answer.

"What news? I pulled the plug on the TV set the day I moved in here."

"Sometime last night," Maxvil said, "Robert Dale was beaten to death in your bed. In your apartment on Irving Place."

4

Styles's hand tightened on the receiver. "What the hell are you talking about, Greg?"

"You did sublet your apartment to Dale, didn't you, Peter?"

"Yes. Through the summer."

"Your cleaning woman, a Mrs. Towers, who seems to have been taking care of Dale while he was there, found him this morning. He had been brutally clubbed to death, apparently in his sleep. No signs of any sort of struggle. We think the killer came over the fence and into the apartment by way of your garden. Dale's skull beaten in like a rotten pumpkin. No way to identify him, legally, except by fingerprints."

"My God, Greg!"

"I'd like it if you'd come back into town," Maxvil said.

"I don't see how I could be of any help," Peter said. "I didn't know Dale at all; friend of a friend. He came to New York to do a play. It's a hit, and he didn't want to stay in a hotel all summer. Since I wasn't going to be using my place I let myself be persuaded—"

"Peter!"

"Yes?"

"The man had thousands of friends, dozens of people connected with that play. The other side of that coin is 'enemy.' We've only just begun the slow business of questioning people. But I've been bothered by something far out."

"Oh?"

"Could someone have thought he was beating you to death in your bed? I think you better come in and talk."

It was a three-hour drive into the city. You drove—and you thought.

Letting Robert Dale have his apartment for the summer

was out of character for Peter Styles. He didn't need the money. Peter's job took him all over the country, all over the world. He had bought the little garden apartment, a co-op on Irving Place, almost ten years ago. It was home base, always there for him to return to without warning or notice. It had not occurred to him until this summer to remove it as an available anchorage.

The problem was that he and Grace had lived there for the seven years of their marriage. She was there now, even though she was dead. A sound at the door, and he would turn, expecting to see her. Much of the time he persuaded himself that reality was a bad dream. Grace would reappear. Things that had been precious to her were still in the apartment, a painting in the living room, little knickknacks she had picked up on their travels, even a small jewel case in his handkerchief drawer. He hadn't been able to persuade himself to remove them. Common sense told him he should sell the apartment and find himself a new place that would have no ghosts. Somehow he hadn't been able to bring himself to it. The nearest thing to escape was to rent the cottage in the Berkshires and finish his book, which might write "The End" to that chapter in his life.

Just around the corner from the Irving Place apartment was The Players, a club for actors, theater people, writers, artists. Once the private home of Edwin Booth, the great nineteenth-century actor, with an interior designed and decorated by the famous Stanford White, the building, which faces Gramercy Park, has been designated a city landmark. To its members, The Players is far from an historical museum of theater paintings and memorabilia. It is a gathering place for men of similar talents and interests, a haven for the famous where they can be shielded from the press and from aggressive fans, a place where super-egos and personal vanities are not catered to by one's peers. It was a kind of home away from home, an island of friendship and affection, of wit and humor, of wisdom and compassion. Peter had been a member for a number of years, and he had been grateful for the shelter it had afforded him in a time of tragedy. He would start for home, the Irving Place apartment, drawn there, yet reluctant, and would stop at The Players, you might say to regroup his strengths with the aid of friends, who knew what he was suffering and yet never once referred to it.

It was there, less than a week ago, that he had met Bob Dale for the first time. He had stopped at the club around midnight, afflicted by the reluctance to hole in at Irving Place. Dale and two or three of Peter's friends were sitting at a round table in the bar. Peter instantly recognized Dale, although they'd never met. It's a strange thing about meeting famous film and television stars; you feel you know them, but you don't. Only the blank look in Dale's eyes reminded Peter that they were strangers.

"Fan of yours," Dale said to Peter when they were introduced. "Look for you in each issue of *Newsview* and if you're not there I throw the bloody thing out."

"I hope you took time to read the review they gave your play," Peter said. "Max Lewis really went overboard for it."

"I always say I never read reviews," Dale said. "Damned lie, of course. Can't wait to get to them. Your man Lewis was particularly generous."

"When Max Lewis gives you superlatives you can count on running for a couple of years," someone said.

"I'm only good for it till October," Dale said. "Film commitment. But I may not last that long if I can't find a place to live."

"Must be thousands of empty apartments in the city during the summer," someone said.

7

Peter had moved to the bar to get himself a drink. Standing there was one of his least favorite people. Every club has one, Peter told himself—relic of another time, hero of another age, endlessly boring about "the good old days." The good old days, Peter had learned, was that time when you had been in the spotlight, center stage. Today is a time when, at best, what you get is reverence for something you once did well but can no longer achieve.

Sam Cowley, Peter had to admit, was an extraordinary man in many ways. Well into his eighties, Sam moved briskly, talked briskly. When he marched to the john he looked like a man on his way to give advice to the president of the United States. Sam had, in fact, been important enough in the entertainment world to dine at the White House fifty years ago. A brilliant and witty playwright in the twenties, he had been chums with such legends as the Barrymores, Pauline Lord, Richard Bennett, Osgood Perkins, and Lee Tracy. He had written plays for some of them. He had been a member of the famous roundtable at the Algonquin Hotel, and he could quote Alexander Woollcott, Dorothy Parker, and Robert Benchley as though they had spoken only yesterday, and not a half century ago. To Sam it still was only yesterday.

Once a master craftsman, a genius at putting together the pieces of character and plot and coming out with a well-made play, Sam Cowley had translated that gift into one of a perpetual meddler in the lives of his friends and acquaintances, moving them around into unwanted situations and confrontations. Characters and plots had brought Sam justifiable fame in the old days. They were his characters and his plots. But now that he was applying those skills to living humans and real situations, people avoided Sam as best they could. Unfortunately, The Players was Sam's home ballpark. He had been a member longer than anyone still living.

8

"Used to put Jack Barrymore to bed upstairs when he'd come in drunk," Sam would say to anyone listening, and he'd be off to a series of anecdotes about the Golden Twenties, some of them, Peter had to admit, very amusing.

Some older men mellow. Sam was cold, brittle, hostile. His pale blue eyes asked perpetual questions: Do you know who I am, how important I am, how unimportant you are in comparison to me?

"You surprise me," Sam said as Peter ordered himself a Jack Daniels on the rocks.

"I thought you were long past being surprised at anything, Sam," Peter said. "But what?"

"You have rented a house in the country for three months," the old man said. "You have an apartment two blocks from here that will stand empty all that time. I would have expected you to jump at the chance to accommodate Bob Dale."

"Accommodate?"

"Let him have your apartment for the summer," Sam said. "He's a good man, an important man."

The old buzzard was at it again, Peter thought. How he knew about the rented cottage in the Berkshires was beyond guessing. It wasn't public knowledge. Keeping it a secret was a part of Peter's plan for uninterrupted work. Sam Cowley spent all his time these days prying into both the important and trivial facts about his acquaintances. It annoyed Peter to be the subject of the old man's impertinent curiosity.

"My maiden aunt from Peoria is taking over the apartment," Peter said.

Sam Cowley gave him a cold look. "You don't have a maiden aunt," he said.

"You have a complete dossier on me, Sam?" Peter asked, curbing his irritation.

"I know everything that's worth knowing about people of any consequence," Sam said.

"I guess I should feel flattered," Peter said, and carried his drink back to the round table.

But Sam, damn him, had started an idea churning. Why not let Dale have the apartment? Perhaps a stranger would exorcise the ghost of Grace. Peter wasn't going to come back to town until his book was finished, come hell or high water.

On impulse he let his hand rest on Dale's shoulder. The actor looked up. "Talk for a minute?" Peter asked.

"Sure."

The two men walked down the grillroom to where two intense, shirt-sleeved members were engaged in a game of eight ball on the pool table.

"It just happens," Peter said, "that I have an apartment around the corner you might like to have. I'm going to be away for three months."

"Oh, brother!" Dale said. "You have no idea what it's like staying in a hotel. I can't walk through the lobby without being surrounded by crazy dames! You're serious?"

"Like to walk around and have a look at it?"

And so they went, walking the two blocks, talking casually about *Triangle,* Dale's play. At Irving Place Peter unlocked the street door and the inner door down the hall and switched on the lights, revealing what had been home for ten years. The minute they were inside he found himself resisting his impulse.

Dale looked at the large living room with its fireplace and walls of bookcases, the kitchenette and small dining alcove, the French doors opening out into the garden that had been Grace's delight. Unguided, he looked into the room beyond with its king-sized double bed where Peter and Grace had loved and slept. Then he turned and eyed Peter steadily,

10

good brown eyes that were suddenly filled with compassion.

"You've changed your mind, haven't you?" he said. "I don't blame you."

Peter turned away, fighting an emotion he had thought was under control.

"I know about your wife, of course," Dale said. "I didn't say anything because what the hell is there for a stranger to say?"

A good man, Sam Cowley had said.

Peter faced him. "The place is yours if you want it."

Dale glanced back at the inner room. "I wouldn't expect to live like a monk, you know. My style might be an intolerable invasion of your privacy."

Dale's understanding of what he was feeling was enough for Peter. "I'd be glad to have you have it," he said.

"It's a marvelous break for me," Dale said. "Right around the corner from The Players, where I have friends. I can't tell you how grateful I am."

He was looking back at the big bed where, in less than a week, he would die, violently.

2

Midafternoon, and Peter found himself in a deserted second-floor card room at The Players with Lieutenant Maxvil, his friend from Homicide, who was in charge of the Dale murder case. The Irving Place apartment, was, for the moment, in the hands of police technicians.

"That's the sum total of my acquaintance with Robert Dale," Peter said, after telling the detective about the night he'd decided, on impulse, to let Dale have the apartment for the summer. "We agreed on a rental, I told him he could move in the day after next, he said good-night, and I never saw him again. We talked on the phone the next day and I arranged for Mabel Towers to clean for him while I was gone. That was it. I don't know anything about him, who his close friends were, his women. Nothing."

Gregory Maxvil was a trim, steel-wire kind of man with penetrating dark eyes that appeared able to read the label on the inside of your shirt collar. He was the new breed of cop, with a law degree and a complete knowledge of all the new scientific approaches to crime fighting. He was a cop who cultivated contacts outside his own city, because New

York, home of the United Nations, is in a sense the capital of the world. Manhattan was his jurisdiction, but he considered the whole world of crime his beat. It was Maxvil's belief that sooner or later the big fish of world crime would come his way, and he was prepared for them.

"There are three immediate possibilities that suggest themselves to me," Maxvil said. "First, someone knew that Dale had sublet your apartment, someone with a motive for violent action against the man."

"I don't suppose he kept it a secret that he'd sublet my place," Peter said. "No reason to. All his friends here at the club must have known."

Maxvil ignored the comment, his eyes narrowed against the smoke from his cigarette. He was a chain smoker. "Second," he said, "is the possibility of a simple thief, looting apartments in that area through the backyard gardens. He hits your place, Dale wakes up and calls out—and that's that."

"And third?"

"Third," Maxvil said, looking straight at Peter, "someone *didn't* know you'd sublet your place to Dale and was out to get you."

"I thought about that driving in," Peter said. "A man in my business makes enemies—but that kind of enemy?" He shook his head. "The thief who got caught in the act seems the most likely, doesn't it?"

"You'd have to go to the morgue and look at the body to believe the fury of the attack," Maxvil said. "Dale wasn't just silenced by a frightened sneak thief. He was annihilated! Clobbered long after he was dead. The killer was in some kind of psychotic frenzy."

Peter's memory played a strange trick on him. The faces of half-a-dozen people who had gone to jail because of his activities as a reporter paraded before him. These were men—and one woman—who might hate him enough to kill him. He had not kept track of any of them or of the eccentricities of the parole system. Which of them might have been free last night, able to come looking for revenge? He told himself it didn't make sense. If he had been the victim, the police would have traced those people in a matter of hours. There would have been a dozen safer ways to polish him off. The answer to Bob Dale's death had to lie in Bob Dale's life.

Maxvil had evidently been thinking along those same lines. "Part of the problem is that Dale's life has been centered on the West Coast," he said. "The police out there are starting to talk to his friends and business associates, but God knows if they'll ask the right questions. People here, people in his play and connected with it, don't know him that intimately. At least they say they don't."

On their way to the empty card room Peter and Maxvil had passed through the bar downstairs. The bar had been crowded with members, all talking about the murder. Peter had noticed that at the center of the group was old Sam Cowley. Something that Sam had said to Peter the night he'd decided to let Dale have his apartment came back to Peter. *"I know everything that's worth knowing about people of any consequence,"* Sam had said.

"There's an old guy downstairs who may know more than he should about Dale," Peter said. He gave Maxvil a thumbnail sketch of the octogenarian playwright.

"Let's see if he'll talk," Maxvil said.

Peter used the card-room phone to call the bar steward to ask for Sam Cowley. The steward returned after a moment to say that the old man was on his way up. Sam was, as usual, reading minds.

Peter went down the hall from the card room to wait for the old man. It took Sam a little time to appear. He came up the stairs from the bar very slowly. Behind him was a white-coated waiter carrying a drink on a tray. The stairs were an effort for Sam, and he looked his age. He wasn't aware that Peter was watching. He took a moment to get his breath, then straightened up, took the dry martini from the waiter, and, at his jaunty best, headed for Peter.

"Thought you'd be sending for me, Peter," he said.

Sam's gray hair, thin on top, was trimmed very short around his ears. His rimless glasses, worn a little low on his pointed nose, forced him to hold his head high to look through them. He looked, Peter thought, like a perky rabbit.

"My friend Lieutenant Maxvil is in charge of the Dale case," Peter said.

"I know," Sam said, walking briskly past Peter and into the card room.

"Pleasure to meet you, Mr. Cowley," Maxvil said. "I'm a great admirer of yours. First Broadway play I ever saw was your *Beggar's Choice*."

Sam gave him a cold look. "You must have been in your diapers," he said. "Let's face it, Mr. Maxvil, that was before you were born."

"I'm afraid it was a revival," Maxvil said.

"Too bad," Sam said. "The original was better. We had actors in those days. Speaking of actors, I take it you want to talk about Bob Dale."

"Please sit down, Mr. Cowley."

Sam raised the glass he was carrying and took a sip of his martini. Then he put the glass down on the round poker table and sat down within reach of it.

"You could say it's providential that you found me here, Lieutenant," Sam said.

"Oh?"

"I am engaged at the moment in writing a book," Sam

16

said. "Six decades of American actors. The Barrymores, Walter Hampden, Osgood Perkins, Lee Tracy, Helen Hayes, Jane Cowl, Katharine Cornell, and on down through the years to Bob Dale. He is my last chapter."

"I thought Dale was more television and films than the theater," Maxvil said.

"God help us, television and films *are* the American actor today," Sam said. "Poor bastards have to eat. Bob Dale, by his performance in *Triangle*, has demonstrated that he didn't have to take a backseat to any of our stage actors. Not that we have so many who are good anymore." The old man lifted his head so that he could look at Maxvil through his glasses. "Your question is, I suspect, who could hate him enough to want to blugdeon him to death?"

"You have an answer to that, Mr. Cowley?"

"I can't name a name," Sam said, "but I know the details of his career, the climate his success created, the people he walked on to get to the top, the women he screwed, the jealous husbands and lovers. Out of that material you can draw your own conclusions, Lieutenant."

Maxvil lit a fresh cigarette and leaned back in his chair. "I'm here to listen, Mr. Cowley," he said.

Sam took another sip of his drink. Someone who would listen was bread and meat and wine to him. Maxvil was an expert at listening. He had learned long ago not to interrupt a witness, try to drag him back onto the main path when he seemed to be deviating. Experience had taught him that in the end he would have to go back and ask questions about something he had distracted his witness from out of impatience. Let them roam; anything might be important. He was the perfect audience for Sam Cowley.

The Dale saga had begun in 1952, according to Sam. The acting bug had bitten Dale in his senior year at Columbia, where he'd been persuaded to play a small part in a production of *The Taming of the Shrew*. At the end of that year he'd signed on as an apprentice in a summer theater in Sharon, Connecticut.

"Not a leading-man type," Sam said, "but a pleasant, homely face that made him ideal for what I think of as Jimmy Stewart juvenile roles. Jimmy was a great juvenile actor before he started to mumble and stutter his way through character roles. Bob Dale had that same, shy charm. Women wanted to mother him, and they got laid for their pains. Women were both his weakness and his strength. He never did marry, which was just as well. He could never have been a one-woman man."

After a season of summer stock Dale set out to make it on Broadway, along with five million other young actors. He didn't have much luck. His résumé showed he had played Shakespeare in college, and he got a couple of extra parts in the Shakespeare in the Park productions. The director of one of those plays was Gavin Hayes, known on Broadway as "the boy wonder." Hayes had a big hit going called *The Lighted Tunnel*. When a national company was formed to tour the country Hayes gave Bob Dale a part in it, a good part.

"They called Gavin Hayes 'the boy wonder,' " Sam said, with a bitter little smile, "but there is some question as to whether or not he is an authentic male." Sam sipped his drink. "No question about Bob's maleness, however. That led to a question. Was our Robert willing to resort to some kind of blackmail to further his career? Interest you, Lieutenant?"

"If you answered the question," Maxvil said.

"No proof in the Hayes case," Sam said. "No factual proof. But Dale certainly managed to use people of importance to get to the top. Most people assumed it was just charm and his special effectiveness with women—in the

18

hay. I still wonder about Hayes, but I have no proof of blackmail. However, after a year on the road in *The Lighted Tunnel,* Hayes, who had gone to Hollywood to make a film, sent for Bob and gave him a rather good part. The question still waits there for an answer. Bob Dale wasn't that good yet. Hayes could have found dozens of young actors better equipped at the time than Bob. He chose Bob. Makes you wonder." Sam smiled his conspiratorial smile and emptied his martini glass. "I wonder if you'd call the bar, Peter, and ask them to send up one of my extra-dry specials?"

The old bastard was just gossiping, Peter thought, and yet—where there's smoke there's usually fire. He put in the order for Sam's drink.

"Up to then," Sam was saying, as Peter came back from the phone, "Bob's career had been ordinary, might not really have existed without Gavin Hayes's interest, whatever the reason for it. But that Hollywood film lifted it into its second and most important phase. The star of that film was Fay Douglas." Sam looked from Maxvil to Peter, obviously expecting some sort of comment.

Down through the history of films there have been the great glamour queens—Garbo, Crawford, Shearer, for example. In the fifties Fay Douglas rated with the greatest of them. A blonde with provocative blue eyes, high cheekbones, a sensuous mouth, an unmatched figure, and a husky, irresistible voice. The film she was in didn't have to be good, she was all that mattered to her audience. She was as different from Crawford as Crawford was from Garbo. Each was unique, each a very special presence up there on the screen. Their private lives were their own, protected by the studios because of their huge investments in their stars—at least until after they were gone. Crawford, since her death, has been revealed as a monster by her own chil-

19

dren. Garbo and Fay Douglas, still living, remain untouched—except by gossip. Sam Cowley was evidently brimming with it. He was disappointed that no one asked for it, but he came through anyway.

"It's not secret," Sam said, "that Fay Douglas was a sex maniac. When she met young Robert Dale she'd already had four husbands and was involved in a torrid affair with one of Hollywood's top male stars. Bob Dale put everyone else out of her mind. Once she had made love with him she was lost. That's how good our Robert was. She fought to have his part built up in that first film. She never went anywhere in public without him, nor in private either, for that matter. It was a tempestuous affair and it lasted for about a year and a half. After that first film Fay insisted that Bob be her leading man in the next one. The studio resisted the idea of starring an unknown, but Fay was not to be denied. That film was *Bitter Torrent,* and Bob Dale was suddenly a huge box-office success. He was made for life. He chose that moment to walk out on Fay and leave her flat." Sam waited for the question from Maxvil that didn't come. He sighed. "You don't do that to a star of Fay's magnitude unless you are a star of equal importance. That's what Bob Dale had suddenly become. Oh, the talk! Oh, the joy of all the women who hated Fay's guts! I suspect she was pretty impossible to live with. Someone has written that Joan Crawford's men had to be both bull and butler. I suspect Fay was in the same category. Her man had to be a lover and a servant. Once he had it made, Bob Dale wanted no more of that.

"The studio had a new film for them. It was a box-office natural after *Bitter Torrent.* Fay refused, flatly, to have Bob as her leading man. It was Fay who was replaced, and an unknown appeared opposite Bob. Jane was also his new woman in private. 'You can't work with a woman without making love to her,' Bob said to some Hollywood character, who repeated it. 'It would destroy your concentration on the job.'

"Fay, of course, got herself another boyfriend and flaunted him all around town. She had vicious comments to make about Bob Dale to anyone who would listen. She gave interviews to the gossip columnists in which she announced that Bob Dale was a lousy actor as well as a lousy human being. The current boyfriend encountered Bob in a Hollywood bar and, deciding to make good marks with Fay, took a swing at Bob. Bob beat him up rather badly. With Fay's support, the boyfriend brought suit against Bob for assault and battery. The suit was lost. Bob gave a rather gracious interview to Sally Thomas, Hollywood's gossip queen, in which he had nice things to say about Fay as an actress, and nothing at all to say about her as a person, good or bad. Whether that tactic was calculated, or whether Bob was just a genuinely nice guy, the result was to increase his popularity with the public enormously. No kiss-and-tell guy he! But it did nothing to heal poor Fay's wounds. Her career and box-office appeal declined as rapidly as Bob's mounted. You may recall that at that time Fay was hospitalized. Her friends tried to cover for her, but the truth would out. She had tried to kill herself with an overdose of sleeping pills."

The waiter appeared from the bar with Sam's second martini. He waited for Sam to taste it.

"Tell Richard," Sam said in a cold voice, "this isn't quite up to par." The waiter reached for the glass. "But it will do. I'm rather too thirsty to wait for him to try again."

Peter was not equipped with Maxvil's patience. "How long ago was this Fay Douglas saga, Sam?"

"Ten years," Sam said, and sipped his drink like a man who found it perfect.

21

The old sonofabitch, Peter thought. What could a ten-year-old love affair have to do with the murder, today, on Irving Place? Sam was just trying to hold stage now that Maxvil had given him the chance. Peter wanted to tell the old man to get to something current, but it was Maxvil's ballgame, and the detective just sat waiting, eyes narrowed against the smoke from his cigarette.

"It was about that time, a year after Fay's suicide attempt, that Bob made a pilot for a television show. It turned out to be 'Casanova Smith.' As you must know, it became one of the most popular and long-running shows on the tube, ranking right along with 'The Mary Tyler Moore' show and 'All in the Family.' Bob was finally making about ninety thousand dollars an episode, ranking him only just behind Carroll O'Connor. Eight years the show ran, and Bob could have quit working when it finished and lived off the residuals for the rest of his life. In that time he slept through all the choice pieces in Hollywood, and half the housewives in America wished they had the chance. A lover who could make you laugh while he made the earth move. If I could make you a list of all Bob Dale's women, Lieutenant, there would be a matching list of men who hated his guts."

"Enough for what happened last night?" Maxvil asked, his first question.

"Who knows," Sam said, and took another sip of his drink. Obviously he wasn't finished.

"Go on, Mr. Cowley," Maxvil said.

"The music goes round and round," Sam said. "Bob could afford to wait for something good when 'Casanova Smith' came to an end. It came up in the form of a play, *Triangle*. Can you guess who offered Bob the starring part, who produced and directed the play?"

"Gavin Hayes, the onetime boy wonder," Maxvil said.

22

"I'm up on the present, Mr. Cowley."

"Are you indeed, Lieutenant?" Sam said. "Do you know about Deborah Wallace?"

"Leading lady in *Triangle*," Maxvil said.

"What else do you know about her?" Sam was clearly annoyed at Maxvil's getting into the act.

"Attractive redhead in her early thirties," Maxvil said. "I talked to her this morning."

"Did you indeed?" Sam said. Maxvil was suddenly one up on him. "How did she take the news?"

"Badly," Maxvil said. "She was naturally shocked."

"I should think so," Sam said. "You remember what I told you about Bob? He couldn't work with a woman without taking her into his bed. Destroyed his concentration otherwise."

"So Deborah Wallace was sleeping with Dale," Maxvil said. "She was his mistress."

"An old-fashioned term, Lieutenant. Not used in the 1970s."

"Are you suggesting that there is a jealous man connected with her?" Maxvil asked.

Sam beamed at the detective. "Her husband," he said.

"There is a Mr. Wallace?"

"Wallace was Deborah's maiden name," Sam said. "Her husband's name is Gavin Hayes." The old man gave Maxvil a triumphant look.

"I thought you said the boy wonder was a gay," Maxvil said.

"It would appear that Gavin is ambidextrous," Sam said.

3

The Irving Place apartment seemed almost strange and unfamiliar to Peter when he went there with Maxvil. It was occupied by the police. Fingerprint men were still at work. Photographers were in the bedroom with other plainclothes detectives. It was no longer home. It was "the scene of the crime."

Sergeant Burke, Maxvil's right-hand man, whom Peter knew from past encounters, greeted them.

"I was just about to send out the Marines for you, Lieutenant," Burke said. "We're nearly through here."

Peter didn't ask, but he assumed that, thank God, the medical examiner's people had long since removed the body. He wasn't prepared, however, for the bloodied sheets on the big double bed. The place where Peter and Grace had made love looked like the scene of a pigsticking—blood everywhere.

"Fingerprints?" Maxvil asked.

"Quite a few," Burke said, "some we can identify, some not. Dale's in this room, the bathroom, the kitchenette, the bar table. You'd expect that. He lived here. Mrs. Towers, the cleaning woman, let us take her prints so we could match them. A few of hers, scattered around as you'd expect. Another person left prints here—bedside table, bathroom, on an unwashed drinking glass in the kitchenette. Dale's on a drinking glass, too. No clue to this other person, unless—" Burke hesitated, glancing at Peter.

"Woman?" Maxvil asked.

"Could be," Burke said. "Sorry to have to pry into your privacy, Mr. Styles, but that closet across the room—"

Peter knew what was coming. He had removed all his personal belongings, clothes, everything of his, to make way for Dale. But he hadn't touched that far closet. He had waited a year and a half to clean it out and couldn't. In it were some dresses, a negligee, a terry-cloth robe that had belonged to Grace.

"Some of my late wife's things," he said in a low, unsteady voice. "Dale said he wouldn't need that closet."

"I had that figured," Burke said, not unkindly. "But there is a black lace negligee there that I wonder about. Different size from the others. Initials. Your wife's name was Grace, wasn't it?"

"Yes."

"The embroidered initials on this black negligee are D.W.," Burke said.

"Deborah Wallace," Maxvil said. "Your Mr. Cowley's gossip would appear to have been accurate, Peter." He turned to Burke. "Leading lady in Dale's play, rumored to be sleeping with him. Seems she was."

"Speaking of the play," Burke said, "you were trying to reach the producer this morning—Gavin Hayes?"

"The lady's husband," Maxvil said.

Burke didn't react. "He phoned in. Will make himself available anytime you want to talk to him. Left a number to call."

26

Maxvil looked around for an ashtray for his cigarette. "Be useful to prove out the lady's fingerprints," he said, "but I'd not like her to know we're thinking about her. *Triangle* is playing—was playing—they won't go on with it, will they, Peter?"

"I should think not. Dale was the attraction."

"If they haven't cleaned house there already, you should be able to pick up the lady's prints in her dressing room," Maxvil said to Burke.

"Incidentally, Hayes called you from his office in the Boswell Theater."

"Maybe we can keep him busy while you go over the lady's dressing room," Maxvil said. "Give Hayes a call and ask him to come down here, Sergeant. When you go up to the Boswell Theater, see if anyone knows where Deborah Wallace went after last night's performance. I had no reason to ask her when I talked to her early this morning. I'd like to hold off putting the question to her until we know a little more. Has the M.E. come up with a time of death, Sergeant?"

"Still vague," Burke said. He'd moved to the door. Peter guessed the bedside phone had prints on it, perhaps not yet photographed. "Dale's play finishes about ten thirty—early curtain. Takes a while for him to get out of costume and makeup, people come backstage to see him. If he came straight home it would have been after eleven. I have Johnny Wolfe checking. Actors tend to stop somewhere for something to eat after a show—Sardi's or someplace like that. Dale apparently hit The Players quite often, but not last night. He did have drinks here with, I now suppose, the lady. They may have eaten something here—crackers and cheese, snack food. Analysis of the stomach should tell us, and perhaps give us an accurate time. The M.E. guesses sometime between two and five was when he got slugged.

Mrs. Towers found him at ten this morning. The M.E. thinks he'd been dead between eight and five hours."

"Deborah Wallace could tell us," Maxvil said. "I want to be sure about her before I ask her straight out."

"Where did you see her this morning?" Peter asked.

"Her apartment. East Thirty-eighth Street—Murray Hill section."

"Hayes wasn't there?"

"Wasn't there. No husband was mentioned. I asked her if she lived there alone and she said she did. She went hysterical when I told her the news, and I didn't like leaving her alone."

"Subletting from someone?"

Burke shrugged. "Her name and address are in the phone book. It seemed rather permanent to me." He turned back toward the living-room phone again. "Where do you want to meet Hayes?"

"Here," Maxvil said. "As soon as possible."

Maxvil's men were convinced that the murderer had come into the apartment through the garden. The front door had not been forced or the lock picked. The garden was the only alternative.

The garden was about thirty feet deep and fifteen wide, surrounded by a ten-foot-high board fence. There was no gate or other means of entrance through that fence. If you were coming in that way, you'd have to come over the top of the ten-foot barrier. That would require considerable agility, according to Sergeant Burke. There was an alley that ran the length of the block behind a series of garden areas. The alley was paved with concrete and revealed no trail of any sort. Burke guessed the intruder could have found something to stand on to help him over the fence, but if he had, he'd later removed whatever it was.

"He didn't have to have anything to get out," Burke explained to Maxvil and Peter. "All he had to do was walk out the front door. He could have gone around back after that and removed whatever he stood on to get in."

"Unless he's the athletic type," Maxvil said. "An agile man could have managed without anything."

Burke had searched the top of the board fence and found a place at the far end where dust and soot had been wiped cleaner than on any of the rest of the surface. He had hoped for something else—a piece of cloth torn from a suit, fingerprints left by the killer as he clung to the top of the fence. There was nothing.

"He carried the weapon in and out with him," Burke said. "No sign of anything in the apartment or the garden he could have used. The M.E. thinks they may find traces of metal or wood in the wound, which would tell us something—I hope!"

"Isn't it possible the murderer just came to the front door, rang the bell, and was let in by Dale?" Peter asked.

"And with a killer in the house Dale went back to bed and went to sleep?" Maxvil asked. He shook his head. "You're thinking it could have been the lady, a regular visitor who actually kept clothes here? Peter, you haven't, as the saying used to go, 'viewed the remains.' The violence of the attack seems to rule out—"

" 'Hell hath no fury—' " Peter said.

Burke didn't buy it. "Someone came over the back fence," he said. "Picture a five-foot-two, hundred-and-ten-pound woman leaping over a ten-foot fence while carrying a bludgeon, smashing in her lover's skull, and walking out the front door, spattered with blood. Maybe you can, Mr. Styles, I can't."

"I think perhaps we can't wait to confront Miss Deborah Wallace," Maxvil said. "Peter's right, you know, Sergeant.

Rage can make a small child unnaturally strong, if adrenaline is pumping.''

It was, however, Gavin Hayes, the onetime boy wonder, who came to them first. He arrived at Irving Place less than twenty minutes after Burke called him.

The chronology, as supplied by Sam Cowley, had to make Hayes a man in his late forties at the least, but he didn't look it. He wore his blond hair in a crew cut, a style that had been popular more than twenty years ago when he'd been at the first high point in his brilliant career. About six feet tall, with pale blue eyes and a trim body that looked as if he spent time in a gym somewhere. Those eyes were set in a handsomely boned face. His speech was cultivated, almost affected, Peter thought. He spoke very softly, like someone in a church or a funeral parlor.

"Terrible thing to happen in your place, Styles," he said, after being introduced to Peter.

"Terrible thing to happen anywhere," Peter said.

The living room had been undisturbed by the violence. Hayes sat down in an upholstered wing chair and looked up, defensively, Peter thought, at Maxvil, Burke, and Peter, who surrounded him.

"I don't know how I can possibly help you," he said.

"I appreciate your coming," Maxvil said. "You must have your own problems, replacing Dale in your play."

"Oh, there's no replacing Bob," Hayes said. "He was one of a kind. We're setting up the machinery for refunding to advance-sale ticket holders. God, how I hate to see money going out instead of coming in."

"I know something about Dale's history as an actor," Maxvil said. "You would appear to have been the first person to have given him a chance, some twenty-odd years ago. Shakespeare in the Park, was it?"

30

"Twelfth Night," Hayes said. "He was what you might call a spear carrier."

"But he struck you as talented?"

The pale blue eyes shifted away from the detective. "I don't know that I gave him much thought. He was just one of a group of extras."

"But you thought enough to hire him for the national company of your play *The Lighted Tunnel,"* Maxvil said.

This, Peter knew, was a key question. Sam Cowley had hinted that Bob Dale had had something on Hayes and had used it.

Hayes's face was an unreadable mask. "Equity, the actors' union, calls for open auditions when you're casting," he said. "Bob came and read. He was good. He had to remind me about the *Twelfth Night.* I hired him because I thought he was the best among those who auditioned. He played the show on the road for a year. Great training for him. He grew, as an actor, in that year."

"And then," Maxvil said, casually, "you sent for him to play a part in a Fay Douglas film called *Bitter Torrent."*

Hayes's thin mouth moved in a sardonic little smile. "My first Hollywood film," he said. "I wanted some people around me I knew, whose work I could expect and trust. They—they try to give a newcomer in Hollywood the business, especially a newcomer with a reputation. I was Broadway's wonder boy in those days. Fay Douglas was the top female star in Hollywood, and she didn't trust some Broadway pipsqueak. I needed a few people like Bob around me. He wasn't the only one who'd worked with me before."

Maxvil put out one cigarette and lit another. "After that first film you did a second one starring Dale," he said. "I understand he'd walked out on Fay Douglas and she refused to appear with him."

31

Hayes shrugged. "After *Bitter Torrent* Bob Dale was big enough to carry a picture without Fay Douglas or anyone else. We went with an unknown girl."

Maxvil took a deep drag on his cigarette and let the smoke out in a long sigh. "We've been led to believe that Dale invariably had a romantic, or at least a sexual, involvement with his leading ladies. Do you recall who took Fay Douglas's place in that second film?"

"Of course I recall," Hayes said, his face masklike again. "I married her sometime later."

"Deborah Wallace?"

"My one adventure in the institution of marriage," Hayes said, that sardonic little smile moving his thin lips.

"You are still married to her?"

"Legally," Hayes said, "but we haven't been working at it for three years."

Maxvil's tone was dramatically casual. "Are you aware that your wife had been having an affair with Dale during the run of *Triangle?*"

"Of course," Hayes said, without hesitation or emotion. "You were right, Lieutenant. Bob couldn't work head on with any woman without getting her into his bed—or himself into hers. Second time around for Debbie—that first film before we were married, this play after we'd been separated for three years."

"Not on-going while you were married—or working at marriage?"

Hayes's laugh was mirthless. "Bob walked out on Debbie after that first film. He got his TV series then, 'Casanova Smith.' Different leading lady in each episode—eight seasons of thirty-nine weeks each! By my count that's three hundred and twelve women. No time for anything permanent. Debbie and I weren't married until Bob was two seasons into 'Casanova Smith.' I wasn't con-

32

cerned with her past romances. After three years of separation I'm not concerned with her present love life." He gave Maxvil an almost disarming smile. "I think I begin to get the drift of this, Lieutenant. Cuckolded husband named Gavin Hayes sneaks into this apartment, and in a jealous rage, brains Robert Dale. Is that how the script reads, Lieutenant?"

"One version of it," Maxvil said quietly.

"You're asking me for an alibi?" Hayes asked.

"For when, Mr. Hayes?"

"From eleven fifteen last night until the early hours of this morning," Hayes said. He actually sounded, Peter thought, as though he was suddenly enjoying himself.

"How do you know the times?" Maxvil asked.

"Bob and Debbie left the Boswell Theater last night at eleven fifteen together. I gather Bob had been dead for some hours when the cleaning woman found him."

"How do you come to 'gather' that?" Maxvil asked.

"Debbie and I are still good friends," Hayes said. "She called me this morning after you'd talked to her, Lieutenant, to tell me what was cooking."

"So do you have an alibi?" Maxvil asked.

"It's right out of a detective story, Lieutenant," Hayes said, actually grinning. "I left the theater about eleven forty-five, after checking the box-office receipts with my man there, stopped in at Sardi's for a couple of drinks, talked to a few people there, went home at a little before one. My apartment is in a remodeled brownstone. No doorman, no elevator man, nobody to verify that. I woke at my usual time, about nine thirty; shaved, bathed, dressed, and went to the office. Debbie called me about eleven thirty with the news. So, no alibi. But that's how it was."

"You find this all amusing?" Maxvil asked. Peter saw he was angry.

"In a way," Hayes said. "It's all so pat—and so absurd. If I'd decided to kill Bob, for whatever reason, it wouldn't have been last night or in the immediate future."

"Oh?"

"I have a big investment in *Triangle*," Hayes said. "Bob was my guaranty of making it back—and a profit. I'd have waited till after I'd recouped to kill him—if I had it in mind."

"And did you have it in mind?"

"Hell, Lieutenant, he was my meal ticket! I like to eat."

"Did your marriage break up because your wife had picked up again with Dale?"

"No. He was still doing his TV thing in Hollywood when we split. She hadn't seen him in all the time we were together."

"Yet you hired them to be in your play, knowing what might happen."

Hayes shifted in his chair. "I think it was Somerset Maugham who said, in effect, that he was one-quarter normal and three-quarters gay. I'm afraid that description fits me, Lieutenant. I simply wasn't equipped for a marriage, so I threw in the towel. What Debbie did with her sex life after that just didn't concern me. They were box office together on the stage. It was good business for me. That's all that mattered."

4

Whether you accepted Gavin Hayes's story about his own activities, his own possible motivations, he was certainly a gold mine of information about Robert Dale's career, about whom the actor had slept with, about who had hated his guts for stealing away a woman, about careers he had injured. And to give Hayes credit, about careers Dale had helped and nurtured. The broad picture of Dale was of a complete professional at the business of acting, untemperamental, generous with his help. He had been, it appeared, Mr. Nice Guy—if he wasn't interested in your woman.

"He was something of a rare bird," Hayes told Maxvil after what seemed like hours of talk, during which Maxvil had made a list of names as long as his arm. "He was no conventional romantic. He never professed undying love to his women, never suggested marriage, never used the word 'forever.' Sex was his favorite sport. All he offered his women was fun, and believe me, they went for it hook, line, and sinker."

"Some of them must have wanted more after they got involved," Maxvil said. "Fay Douglas, I understand, never forgave him for walking out on her, and finally attempted suicide because of him.''

"Poor Fay. A hopeless egomaniac. No one could walk out on the great Fay Douglas. No one ever had till Bob Dale came along. She did the walking out. But Bob didn't play his usual game with Fay. He was fighting to make a name for himself in Hollywood when he tangled with her. She was important stuff, big league. She could make a star of him and she did—along with my help as his director, you understand. She made demands on Bob, and he met those demands because he needed her. I think anyone, before or since Fay, who asked more from him than fun and games found him gone with the wind. I've heard women say he was heartless, but I've never heard anyone say he was a lousy lover—except Fay, who was obviously lying through her teeth. She wanted him so badly you could smell it.''

Men? There were plenty of men who hated Bob Dale. Producers, directors, male stars who had always had the cream of the Hollywood crop for the asking. Dale never paid any attention to a no-trespassing sign set up in front of any women.

"He didn't deliberately set out to steal other men's women,'' Hayes said. "It wasn't a challenge. It wasn't a way to satisfy his own ego. If the lady said no, he asked someone else. Women who worked with him rarely said no. They couldn't be exposed to him long and not be mesmerized by his special charm.''

Somewhere, Peter thought, there must be a man who couldn't forgive the theft of his woman. The man's name could be on the list Maxvil had compiled from Hayes's gossip. It would be a long and tedious piece of detective work to pick the right name from that list.

If that was the motive, if that was the answer.

*

"Of course you are the perfect person to cover this story, Peter," Frank Devery said. "Man murdered in your apartment, in your bed."

Devery is the publisher and editor of *Newsview Magazine,* the biggest-selling newsmagazine on the stands. He is Peter Styles's closest friend. He is a short, stocky man, with sandy brown hair and bright, inquisitive eyes. Outsiders saw him as an abrasive, slave-driving kind of a man, but people who knew him were aware that beneath the surface was a genuine compassion for people, that he would go all the way out to the end of the limb for what he called his "family." His family were the people who worked for him at *Newsview,* from Peter Styles down to the newest and lowest-ranking copyboy in the printing plant. He was a fighter for justice as well as for his friends. His reporters knew they could count on his support. He had often said, *"I know every damn word that's printed in my magazine and I stand back of every one of them."* Somebody had made an affectionate quip about him at the office, based on a television commercial: "We don't have a piece of the rock here at *Newsview.* We have the rock itself."

"You promised me when I took the cottage up the line," Peter said to his friend and boss.

It was early evening, but Peter had found Devery still in his office in the Newsview Building on Madison Avenue. The Irving Place apartment was finally free of police, but Peter hadn't wanted to stay there. He owed it to Devery to tell him what he knew about the Dale case, to supply the reporter who would cover the story with as much of the background as he and Maxvil had been able to collect from Sam Cowley and Gavin Hayes.

"I know I promised to let you alone till you'd finished your book," Devery said. "But you brought this to me, friend, not the other way around."

"I couldn't refuse to help Greg Maxvil," Peter said. "He could have issued a warrant for my arrest if I had."

"In addition to being your friend, he's no dummy," Devery said.

One of the features of Devery's office was a refrigerator. All it ever contained was cooling beer, a couple of bottles of wine, and an ice-making gadget. Hard liquor was kept in a cabinet next to it. Devery was pouring Jack Daniels on the rocks for both of them.

"Drink and think," Devery said, handing a glass to Peter.

"You've got good people out on the Coast," Peter said. "That's where the Dale story probably is."

"A hell of a lot of it seems to be here," Devery said. "Hayes, Deborah Wallace—very active parts of Dale's life, very currently involved."

Peter took a swallow of his drink. "I'd have been out of this business long ago, Frank, if I didn't have an instinct for a story when it broke. I listened to Gavin Hayes talk about Dale, and himself, and his wife for a couple of hours. I came away pretty well convinced that Hayes isn't a killer."

"And the girl?"

"I haven't seen her or talked to her, of course."

"Some woman that Dale walked out on was bound to blow her stack sooner or later." Devery reached for a cigar in a cedar-lined humidor on his desk. "Men of our age have a tendency to assume that women can't commit violence like this. After thirty years in the news business I don't buy that any longer. Maybe women tend to commit more subtle crimes, but they are quite capable of going violently nuts!"

"Maxvil's problem," Peter said. "Frank, I need to get this book out of my system. I need to get free of the whole business, once and for all. I don't even want to go back to my own apartment, my own home."

38

"You and your instinct for a story!" Devery said. He lit his cigar and smoke swirled around his head. "You're overlooking the most obvious reason you should be interested in this one."

"What, for instance?"

Devery put his glass down hard on the desk. "You dumb clod, you could have been the intended victim!"

"I don't think so," Peter said.

"Your instinct tells you that? So you go back to the Berkshires and your book. The whole damn world will know tomorrow where you are. You're part of the Dale story; it was your apartment. So the man who made a mistake finds you and rectifies it. You just going to let him come and get you? My instinct tells me he just might do that."

"Who?" Peter asked. It was a theory he didn't want to buy.

"Go through the office files if you can't remember for yourself," Devery said. "There are damn near as many people who hate your guts for what you've dug up about them as Dale had women!"

Reluctantly, Peter had to admit there was some truth in what Devery said. A campaign against terrorism both in this country and abroad had made him some particularly dangerous enemies; dangerous because they were impersonal. People in various power groups were in jail because of Peter's investigative skills. The mind of the terrorist is concerned only with revenge. They were faceless because there was no way of knowing who they might be. The murder of his wife, Peter knew, with bitterness, was an act of revenge against him. He had brought those particular heartless killers to justice, but he knew that those killers had friends, and those friends had friends. It could go on and on, Peter knew, move and vicious countermove.

Devery watched his friend, guessing what was going on behind his expressionless face.

"Maybe," Devery said, "you can sleep at night, knowing that it's possible someone connected with your past may have beaten Robert Dale to death in your dark bedroom thinking he had you. Maybe you can, but bear in mind that I can't, and Maxvil can't, and none of your friends can. We care about you, chum."

"Thanks," Peter said.

"You can't write a book with a gun beside your typewriter," Devery said. "Good as you are, you have to concentrate on what you're doing—one thing at a time. If the killer meant to get you, none of us can help you without your help. If he meant to get Dale, you'll have no peace until it proves out. If you decide to get sensible and protect your own hide, you're the best man to cover the story for *Newsview*."

Logic, when you don't want to be convinced, is bitter medicine. Ever since Grace's death he had been operating like a car with one wheel half-locked. Isolation in the Berkshires and finishing his book had been set up to free that locked wheel. But Devery was right. You couldn't concentrate on a creative job with a gun at the ready and you wondering about your personal safety.

"You have to be the hunter, not the hunted," Devery said. "You can't live on the run, Peter. It's out of character for you. And to just sit still and do nothing would be like running. Either someone had a motive for killing Dale, knew where to find him, and did it—or it was a mistake, and you can expect a night visitor tomorrow, the next day, the week after. You can't function without answers, Peter."

Peter lifted his glass, drained it, and put it down on the table beside his chair.

"Where do I start?" he asked.

*

Most Homicide detectives would scream their heads off at the thought of an investigative reporter messing around in a case they were handling. Perhaps it couldn't be prevented—the reporter had his job to do—but any sort of cooperation was handled very close to the vest.

Peter's relationship with Greg Maxvil was different. They had worked together before. Maxvil knew that nothing he revealed to Peter would appear in print until he gave the word; that anything Peter unearthed would come his way. The result was an open and unsuspicious collaboration.

"I'm glad you decided to get your feet wet," Maxvil said when Peter told him he'd decided to cover the case for Devery. "It means you'll be keeping your eyes peeled for what may be a danger to you."

"You and Devery both seem to feel that's likely," Peter said.

"At least until we get some sort of solid lead that convinces us that Dale was the intended victim," Maxvil said. "So far the Cowley-Hayes gossip club has provided us with almost too many leads. It will take months to check them out." He made an impatient gesture. "Hundreds of women Dale loved and left. Hundreds of men who hated him for stealing from them. I'd have to hire an army to follow up on all of them."

"Somewhere there has to be someone who knows something factual that would eliminate most of those people," Peter said.

"Deborah Wallace," Maxvil said. "I was about to turn the heat on when you called me."

They were having a late snack in a little Italian restaurant around the corner from Irving Place. Pietro's was a place Peter went to when he didn't want to run into people he knew; good Italian cooking, good wine, good bread and cheese. Pietro knew who Peter was, but he didn't identify him to his neighborhood clientele. He knew Peter came there for privacy.

"The Wallace woman was Dale's lover fifteen years ago, and again, now, in the present," Maxvil said. "We have to assume she was there last night, for awhile at least. Burke matched up fingerprints he lifted in her dressing room at the theater with ones we found in the apartment—the bedside table, the bathroom, the unwashed drinking glass in the kitchenette. It was a going affair. He must have talked to her about what was current in his life."

"But you haven't asked?"

"When you phoned me that you were going to take a hand I thought it might be a starting point for you," Maxvil said. "She was hysterical when I talked to her this morning. She's the kind of person who's terrified of cops. She might talk to you, a friend of Dale's."

"He wasn't a friend. I didn't know him at all."

"Friend enough to let him have your apartment. Member of his club. A man who wonders whether the violence was meant for him and not Dale. You need her help for your own sake."

And so it was that Peter got to meet Deborah Wallace that night. Maxvil had her number, culled from the phone book. A husky but unsteady voice answered Peter's ring. He told her he was Peter Styles of *Newsview*. She sounded frightened.

"I'm afraid I can't talk to reporters, Mr. Styles. Not yet, anyway. I—I'm far too done in—"

He told her he wasn't really calling as a reporter. He told her he was concerned for his own safety. It was possible, if they could talk, that she would remember something that might help him.

"I don't remember Bob talking about you, Mr. Styles, except to say how nice it was of you to let him have your place."

"I would sleep better if I could convince myself the murderer wasn't after me," he told her. "I need your help, Miss Wallace."

Perhaps she needed to talk to someone. Perhaps her curiosity was piqued. She invited him, despite the fact it was almost eleven at night, to come to her apartment on Thirty-eighth Street.

Peter had never seen Deborah Wallace on the screen or on stage. Maxvil said she was "in her early thirties." She had to be at least that, if she had been Dale's lover fifteen years ago. He wondered what to expect as he waited in the foyer of the remodeled brownstone after ringing the bell under her name. Almost instantly the lock clicked in the front-door mechanism. Peter let himself into the dimly lit interior. The husky voice he'd heard on the phone called down the stairwell to him.

"One flight up, Mr. Styles."

She was waiting for him at the door of the back apartment on the second floor. The hall lighting was so poor that the only impression he had at first was of a medium-tall, very erect woman with dark red hair that probably wasn't its natural color; her face neutralized by large, shell-rimmed, black glasses. When you can't see eyes, you really have no concept of what the face is like. She was wearing a navy-blue housecoat that hung, loosely, from broad shoulders and obliterated her figure—if she had one.

"Thank you for letting me come, Miss Wallace," Peter said as he reached her.

"Come in, Mr. Styles." She stood aside to let him pass her into a brightly lit living room. He was conscious of air conditioning, which was a relief from the humid summer evening.

It was a pleasant large room, furnished in early American. The person responsible was a person of taste. The only unusual feature was one wall completely covered with

43

photographs, all autographed, of people Deborah Wallace had worked with in films and on the stage. Some he recognized. There was one of Robert Dale, given no preferential position in this gallery of actors. He noticed Henry Fonda, and Fay Douglas, and Paul Newman, and half-a-dozen other stars, old and new. Deborah Wallace had had a career if she'd worked with all these people.

"Friends," she said in that intriguing, husky voice. She gestured to a tastefully upholstered wing chair. "Can I get you a drink—or some coffee?"

He noticed that she was wearing silver sandals, and that her toenails were nicely manicured and lacquered a pale pink.

"I didn't come here to sponge on you, but a drink would be fine," he said. "It's been a long day."

"Oh, God!" she said. Her mouth was wide and it trembled a little at the corners. "Bourbon? Scotch? Gin?"

"Bourbon on the rocks just might save my life," Peter said. He sat down in the big chair.

She went off into the kitchen and he heard the sound of ice cubes being broken out. He was trying to guess how to begin with her. She had not been just a one-night stand with Bob Dale. Fifteen years ago they had been lovers while they made a film together. It had picked up again, recently, probably during the rehearsals of *Triangle* and the three weeks it had been running on Broadway. She had been with Dale the night before, after the play, at Irving Place. These were old friends, intimate friends; there must have been endless talk about mutual friends, about working crises. If Dale had had a recent run-in with anyone, he'd almost certainly have mentioned it to this woman to whom he was so close.

She came back from the kitchen with a bourbon for him and what looked like a gin and tonic for herself. She sat down in the corner of a couch facing him.

"I don't honestly know how I can be of any use to you, Mr. Styles. As I told you on the phone, Bob only spoke about you once, the first night I went to your apartment with him. Just to say how lucky he was to have run into you at The Players."

Peter gave her his best and warmest smile. "There are two things you can do for me, Deborah. You can call me Peter, and you can take off those black glasses. You're hidden behind them."

She hesitated a moment, and then she reached up and took them off. It was as if an extra light had been turned on in the room. Her eyes were an extraordinary shade of violet. He was reminded of Elizabeth Taylor. They were set wide apart, and the whole structure of her face took on a new form: high cheekbones with little hollows under them, the wide, generous mouth balancing the whole. There was a kind of hurt look in the eyes, almost a plea for help, Peter thought. It was enormously appealing, arousing an impulse to respond to that plea. It took only seconds to realize that she was a very beautiful woman in a very distinctive and individual way. She was not a type, fell into no recognizable category. He regretted that he had never seen her work. She must be electric before the camera or on stage. She was ageless, he thought. She could have been in her late twenties; she had to be in her middle thirties.

"It gets to be a habit to hide from strangers, the public, except when you're appearing before them in your job," she said.

"A loss for them," Peter said. "You've very lovely, Deborah, and that's not small talk."

"Thank you, sir," she said with a little smile.

He tasted his drink. It was a good bourbon. "There's a bad thing about a bad thing like this," he said. "Your pri-

vacy gets ripped away from you. The police and God knows
how many others know that you were having an affair with
Dale. Your negligee in a closet at my place, your fingerprints on a drinking glass in the kitchenette.''

"Is that scandalous—or even unusual in this day and
age?'' she asked. "Everyone without two heads has a sexual involvement with someone.''

"Neither scandalous nor unusual,'' Peter said, "and yet
half the town will be dining out on it. In my case I'd like you
not to think I've been prying into your life to provide myself
with small talk.''

"It hadn't occurred to me,'' she said. "You see, Peter,
your life became public property at the time your wife was
killed. You'd have to be sensitive to my resistance to give
interviews less than twenty-four hours after Bob was—
was— I believed you when you said I might be able to help
you, but I don't know how.''

She reached for a cigarette in a silver box on the table
beside the couch. He stood up and bent over her with his
lighter. Close to her he was aware of a delicate perfume,
distinctive, probably prepared for her alone. Their eyes
met. Damn, he thought, this woman could make you forget
what your immediate purpose was. He went back to his
chair and his drink.

He told her, briefly, what Maxvil and Devery feared. The
killer had come to the Irving Place apartment to get him—
Peter. He had assumed the sleeping figure in the bed was
Peter Styles. In the dark room he had not bothered to make
a positive identification. He had killed and gone away, assuming his mission was accomplished. There were people,
groups, forces who might have wanted to do just that.

"If that is what happened,'' he said, "then I can expect
another go at me. If Robert Dale was the actual target, then
I can relax. But I have to know for sure.''

"But how can I help?" she asked. The smoke from her cigarette made a kind of halo around her dark red hair.

"Lovers talk to each other intimately, casually, unguardedly," Peter said. "Did Dale talk about a recent row with someone? Did he mention the presence of someone in New York with whom he might have had trouble in some other place—Hollywood, for example—at some other time? There has been talk already today that, at some time, Dale may have blackmailed your husband. The combination of that with the fact that you had renewed your affair with Dale has your husband well up on the list of suspects—if Dale really was the intended victim."

She had begun shaking her head from side to side before he had finished what he was saying. It wasn't a vigorous, defensive denial, but almost an amused indication that he was talking nonsense.

"Poor Gavin," she said. "He is probably the least violent man you have ever met, Peter. He would rather be bitten by a fly than kill it. If you had followed his work in films and on stage, you'd know that he never touches today's popular kind of specific violence. He can't bear the sight of blood. I take it, Peter, that you're aware he's gay?"

"Three-quarters gay, he told us. The other quarter, he said, accounts for you."

"And did he tell you that quarter wasn't enough for me?"

"He implied it wasn't enough for him."

"If it pleases him to say that, I don't mind," Deborah said. She put out her cigarette, half-smoked. She hesitated a moment. "You know so much about me, Peter, so you know that Bob Dale and I first got together fifteen years ago. It was in a film called *Rivertown*. The script was written to star Bob and Fay Douglas, with Gavin to direct. Bob had had a thing with Fay and walked out on her. Fay refused to co-star with Bob. I, completely unknown, got the part. It was scaled down to match my—my unknownness, and Bob's part was expanded to make it a starring vehicle for him. I didn't mind. It was my first big break. And—and I was subjected for the first time to Bob's special charm. He was marvelous to work with; generous, patient with my lack of experience before a camera. I know now that this was Bob's way of working with all actors, men and women. He never upstaged anyone, never made it difficult for anyone, like so many stars. Quite the reverse. In our business you can hear endless talk about the bitchiness of stars, but never about Bob. As an actor he was admired, respected, loved. You could fill a book with stories about the way he helped other people in the profession. He would take no nonsense from another performer, but also he never dished out any nonsense of his own. No vanity, no demanding ego."

"A eulogy he may deserve at his funeral," Peter said. "But as a man—away from his work?"

She ignored the question. "He wasn't the only one who helped me in that first film," she said. "Gavin was marvelous, patient with me to a fault. I was twenty, he was thirty, with all the glamour of a big Broadway success surrounding him, and with one big film credit, *Bitter Torrent* with Bob and Fay Douglas. He treated me like a fatherly friend. He knew all the tricks of the trade and he helped me master many of them. I was endlessly grateful to him, amused by his witty scalping of most of the Hollywood bigwigs." She looked away from Peter's direct stare. "He even advised me about my love life."

"Bob Dale?"

She nodded. "Off the set Bob was giving me a rush. I was flattered and a little scared. He was on the rebound from Fay Douglas, I thought, and I could only be a disappointment to him after Fay. I—I was a virgin, believe it or not,

Peter. I could not make him an experienced or sophisticated lover, the kind he'd had in Fay. Gavin advised me, if there wasn't some other man in my life, to let Bob have his way. 'He will teach you things you never dreamed of,' Gavin said, 'so long as you don't insist on his saying "forever" to you. It will remove tensions that are obvious in your work together. You won't be hurt if you don't ask for too much.' '' Deborah looked straight at Peter again. ''And so I said yes to Bob.''

''And Gavin's advice was good?''

She hesitated. ''I find it difficult to talk about it to you, Peter. It—it was so very private, even if it became public knowledge. I was a girl, full of romantic notions. Bob seemed surprised to find that this was the first time for me. But not disappointed, not contemptuous as I was afraid he might be. He was very gentle and tender in the beginning. I thought afterwards that he was like an athletic trainer, preparing someone for the big game, the big race. Without knowing it I was suddenly prepared. And then it was for real; Bob's kind of real that became my kind of real.'' Again she turned her eyes away. '' 'I will tell you, in the act of making love to you,' Bob said, 'that I love you. It is part of the music that goes with the act. But don't interpret it, Debs'—he called me Debs—'as meaning something permanent. I'm fond of you, I like you, which is most important of all, but when the next job comes along and there is someone else in daily contact with me, I'll be gone. If what we now have, without promises, is as much fun for you as it is for me, let's keep on with it while we have it. If it isn't, take off now; because I like you, I don't want to hurt you.' I didn't take off because it was the most fun I'd ever had in my life. Just sex for the pleasure of sex, with no other demands, no other obligations.''

''But you took on demands and obligations when you

49

married Gavin Hayes,'' Peter said.

She took another cigarette from the box on the table and, once again, he bent over her with his lighter, was aware of her fragrance, was disturbed by it.

"After the film with Bob, which took several months in the shooting—we were lovers all that time—it turned out just as Bob said it would. He went on to something else, and someone else. I told myself I was prepared for it, but obviously I wasn't. I told myself he'd educated me to have sex with other men on the same level as it had been with him. But I found I wasn't. I denied to myself that I was in love with Bob, hurt at losing him—because he hadn't wanted me to be 'in love.' Whatever I really felt, I couldn't bring myself to attempt the same kind of relationship with any other man.''

"And there must have been endless opportunities.''

"I'm not unattractive to men," Deborah said.

"Yes, ma'am," Peter said, and grinned at her.

"My best friend was Gavin," she said. "He stayed interested in my career, got me guest shots on TV shows, a couple of films. I used to go to his apartment, cook dinner for him, listen with amusement to his endless gossip about the famous and near-famous people in our profession. It was like being close to another woman. There was never any sex talk about ourselves, but endless rumors and guesses about other people. Bob had started his TV series, 'Casanova Smith,' and the whole community was chattering about him—a new girl every week, with each new episode. Maybe I was envious, but I found I wasn't hurting.

"After almost two years Gavin took off for New York to direct a play. It was one of his few failures and he was back in Hollywood after three months. He said he had missed me more than he'd believed possible. To my amazement he suggested marriage. Well, I enjoyed his company. There

50

was no other man in my life. He was important to my career. I trusted him, his judgments about my future. Oh, I don't know, Peter, it seemed like a friendly thing to do.''

"Even though you knew he was not the great lover.''

"I don't believe I really thought about the sexual aspect of it,'' she said. "I enjoyed his company, I was grateful for his friendship, I needed his help. If he wanted some kind of permanence, it seemed worth a try. I wasn't very bright, I guess. I hadn't dreamed he would be afraid of a sexual intimacy with me. He began to see me as some kind of cannibal, intent on devouring him. In a very short time there was nothing physical between us. But I hung in there for three years. One day he said, 'Thanks for trying, Deborah, but there isn't much point in it anymore, is there?' So, I simply moved out of his apartment and took one of my own. Property laws in California are complex, and since neither of us needed to be free we didn't bother about a divorce. I experimented with a few men, but none of them were Bob Dale. Thank God I was busy and my career was going nicely. Three years drifted by. I did a couple of films for Gavin. Our relationship seemed to be just what it had been before we'd tried being married. Gavin seemed to feel no embarrassment or regrets. He was wonderful to work with. As a director he knew all my pluses and minuses.

"One day he told me that he had a new play he wanted to do on Broadway. He would produce and direct. He wanted Bob Dale, who had just finished eight seasons in 'Casanova Smith,' to star in it, and he wanted me to play the female lead. He gave me a copy of the script to read. It was *Triangle*. The lead was perfect for Bob, the part he wanted me to play was the best I'd ever been offered. I would have jumped at it, except—''

"How would things be between you and Dale?''

She nodded. "Gavin was aware of it. If I wanted to say no to avoid the inevitable, he would understand, but it was something in terms of my career I should consider very seriously. You know why I hesitated?" She gave Peter an almost defiant look. "It had been fifteen years since Bob Dale had introduced me to his kind of pleasure. I'm not a rosy-cheeked girl anymore. Maybe he wouldn't even look at me. There was a nice ingenue part in the play. An attractive young actress would play it."

"Didn't you know that women get better and better as they get older?" Peter asked.

"I shouldn't have worried," she said. "Bob greeted me at the first rehearsal as though fifteen years ago were yesterday. After that first day all he said was, 'My place or yours?' " She sat very still for a moment, her eyes narrowed, as if something she saw in the past were giving her pain. "It was the old, marvelous fun again," she said. "Except there was a difference. I couldn't quite put my finger on it until—until last night. We went to your place—your lovely place. We made love, as always. Afterwards we went into the kitchenette to make drinks. I knew Bob had something on his mind, and I thought I knew what it was. He'd had enough of me! He sat there, looking at his drink, sipping it. 'Do you know,' he said, 'that since our first time together there have been, quite literally, hundreds of women in my life?' I was preparing myself for the blow, but I tried to keep it light. 'According to Hollywood gossip, A to Z and back again,' I said. He looked up at me. 'Would you believe me if I told you that none of them could match you, as a lover, as a person?'

" 'But—?' I said.

" 'No but,' he said. 'Something has happened to me, Debs. Playing the field has lost its appeal for me. I'm in love.'

52

" 'Lucky girl,' " I said.

" 'You damned idiot, Debs, it's you, don't you know that? I want to say the word I forbade you to say years ago. Forever! Did I teach you too well, Debs? Can you never say it?'

"My God, Peter, could I say it! Forever, forever, forever! I had a TV interview to make this morning. The Eileen Carroll show. I had to get rest, get ready for it. I had to look well before the camera. We talked about my legal problems with a divorce.

" 'To hell with property settlements,' Bob said. 'Give Gavin the moon if he wants it. I have more than enough for both of us—forever.'

"We both kept laughing, and saying the forbidden word, and clinging to each other. Today was the day it was to have begun—forever. At ten thirty this morning I was just about to go to my TV show, wondering why Bob hadn't called me, when Lieutenant Maxvil got to me with the news." She broke down, then, crying quietly. Peter waited, resisting the temptation to comfort her. Finally she looked at him, eyes brimming. "I've told you all this, Peter, so that you will see how absurd it is to suspect Gavin, and—and how difficult it is for me to think about anything except that Bob is gone."

"And yet I have to press you for facts," Peter said. "In the fifteen-year gap in your relationship with Dale, did you never see him?"

"Rarely," she said. "Bob hates—hated—going to public places, hated being fawned over by movie and TV fans determined to invade his life. He seldom went to Hollywood restaurants or night spots where other actors go because they want to be seen. We met a few times when we were working at the same studio. He'd almost always be with some other girl, the current one. He'd greet me warmly, kiss me on the cheek, introduce me as 'one of my favorite people and a fine actress,' and that was that. We never had a conversation, no catch-up talk.''

''Until you got together again this time.''

''Maybe I haven't made Bob clear to you,'' Deborah said. ''He was dedicated to the present. He wasn't interested in the past, and, until last night, I thought he wasn't interested in the future. When—when it started over again, at the beginning of *Triangle,* we neither of us talked at all about what had gone on in between. We found each other again with a very special pleasure, we talked a little about the play we were rehearsing, and there was—'' She stopped, her eyes widening. ''In the theater you sign a contract to do a play. Equity, the actors' union, allows the producer to fire you after a few days—four or five days. I'm vague about it, because I'm lucky enough never to have been dropped. After those few days the producer has to honor the contract. There was a character man, Lucien Smallwood, who was hired for *Triangle.* The second day of rehearsal he had some kind of run-in with Bob. That was unusual. Bob never had trouble with other actors. In any case, I think Gavin foresaw trouble the whole run of the play and he dropped Smallwood. Smallwood went screaming around the theater that Bob had gotten him fired, threatening to get even. But surely not—''

''You don't know what the quarrel was about?''

''Bob just said he was a lousy actor and a lousy guy.''

''Had they worked together before?''

''No. I'm sure not. Gavin would know.''

''It's odd Gavin didn't mention this quarrel when we talked to him.''

''I'm probably making too much out of nothing,'' Deborah said. ''I've heard men in my business threaten each other dozens of times—drama, temperament, the big scene. Actors love to play big scenes. But you asked me to remember things—"

"No one else?" Peter asked. "No longtime, running feud?"

"Bob never mentioned any such thing," she said, "and I never heard any rumors of any such thing. Bob was one of the most generally liked actors in the business."

"Except by the men whose women he stole," Peter said.

She gave him an odd little smile. "I'm sure you know, Peter, that men rarely steal women from other men. Most men make it known that they find an attractive woman attractive. It's a politeness, like it used to be to rise when a woman came into the room. It's usually the woman who runs from one man to another. Bob was a pushover, not a pirate."

5

It was nearly one in the morning. The street outside Deborah Wallace's apartment appeared to be deserted. Peter found himself glancing up and down the block, looking for something in the shadows. He suddenly wondered if this was an unconscious habit of his, or whether Devery and Maxvil had gotten to him. Or had the woman upstairs halfway convinced him that Bob Dale could not have been the intended target for the violence that overtook him?

What an irony for Deborah Wallace! A romantic girl, swept off her feet by the glamour boy of her time, taught to expect nothing from him but the pleasure of the moment yet hanging onto a hope for him through an impossible marriage, and then, after fifteen years, finding that her waiting had not been in vain. Tomorrow she would have him forever, but there was to be no tomorrow. Peter hadn't suggested it to her, but her professionalism may have contributed to the tragedy. A contract to film a television commercial requiring her to look and be at her best had taken her away from Dale on the night they had found each other—forever. Neither one of them would have considered ignoring a call to work, no matter how much they would have liked to. They were total professionals at what they did. Bob Dale wouldn't have thought of asking her to forget about the job on that very special night for both of them. It would have been against all the rules of their way of life. Yet, had she stayed, they might have been awake when a killer slipped in from the garden; she might have been awake and screamed a warning.

Or, Peter thought grimly, they might both have been dead.

At the hands of a killer who was after someone else entirely?

He walked west toward Park Avenue, aware of a special alertness. He was listening for the sound of footsteps behind him, looking for some movement in the shadows ahead of him. He actually felt a kind of relief when he reached the better-lighted avenue without incident and was able to flag down a cruising taxi. His objective was The Players. There would still be people in the bar there, people playing eight ball at the pool table or bridge at one of the round tables. Somebody would be able to tell him something about an actor named Lucien Smallwood.

Peter paid off the taxi outside the entrance to The Players on Twentieth Street and went down the two steps from the street level to the front door, illuminated on both sides by lovely old wrought-iron lamps. Tommy, the night man, recognized him as he paused by the coatroom. He could hear voices coming up the stairway from the bar.

"Many people down there, Tommy?" Peter asked.

"Quite a few, sir," the night man said. "Pardon me, Mr. Styles, but is there any news about Mr. Dale?"

"Nothing positive," Peter said.

The last thing Deborah Wallace had asked of him was that he keep the story of that last "forever" moment with Bob

Dale to himself. The gossip mongers would have more of a field day then they already were having if that choice romantic morsel became known.

"Do we have a member named Lucien Smallwood, Tommy?" Peter asked.

"Not that I know of, sir. Would you like me to look at the membership list?"

Peter smiled. "If you don't know him, Tommy, he isn't a member." He started down the winding marble staircase to the bar.

There were a couple of dozen people in the bar. Old Sam Cowley was holding court at one of the round tables. The minute Peter was spotted by someone he was surrounded. By now everyone knew of his closeness to Lieutenant Maxvil and therefore to the case. He had nothing to tell them except that Deborah Wallace had probably been the last person to see Dale alive. It was not loose talk to pass that along. Deborah's relationship with Dale was not a secret.

"Lucky for her she didn't spend the night with him," a voice said at Peter's elbow.

Peter turned and found himself facing Max Lewis, the drama critic for *Newsview*. Peter had known Lewis for some years, though not intimately. They'd sat in together on any number of editorial conferences at the magazine. The dark, rather good-looking critic was not somebody Peter particularly liked. The man's personal vanity was a little too much for him. The handful of men who cover the Broadway scene for the daily papers and a few magazines have a rather dangerous power over the destinies of actors, writers, and producers in the New York theater. Men like Clive Barnes, Richard Eder, and Max Lewis can make or break a play by their comments, written very shortly after an opening night. They can turn on or turn off potential audiences. Peter remembered someone saying that Max Lewis's favorable review of *Triangle* meant that Bob Dale's play was in for a long run. Had his whim of the moment been negative, *Triangle* could have closed after the first week. Lewis was aware of his importance to the theater scene, and he demanded that he be treated like a person of consequence. He always seemed out of place to Peter in a club like The Players, whose membership was three-quarters theater people. It was, Peter thought, like having the hangman present at the jury deliberations involving the death penalty. A hungry hangman.

"She had a TV interview the next morning and she had to be ready for it," Peter said. "I guess you could say that was lucky for her, Max."

"Robbed of a boyfriend," Lewis said, "but almost certainly a coming star. She was awfully damned good in *Triangle.*"

Peter made his way to the bar. Max Lewis stayed with him. It was as if Lewis knew that his connection with Peter, through *Newsview,* gave him an extra importance. Lewis was not a man to hide his light under a bushel. He wore his dark hair long, and his wardrobe was unbelievably flamboyant. Tonight he was wearing a wine-red dinner jacket with a lace-frilled dress shirt and an overlarge red bow tie. He carried a handkerchief up his sleeve, like an eighteenth-century fop. Peter had seen him often at opening nights on Broadway, making a late entrance down the aisle, dressed so unusually that heads turned. His presence must be noted. A peacock fetish, Peter thought.

It is a custom at The Players that no man buys a drink for another. It prevents the embarrassment of not repaying someone for a favor if you can't afford it.

Peter ordered a Jack Daniels on the rocks, and the bartender slid the chit across the bar for him to sign. You didn't pay in cash. Actors out of work are often broke. Lewis reached for the slip.

"On me," he said, and signed with a flourish.

"I can afford it, Max," Peter said.

"Expense account," Lewis said, giving Peter a sardonic smile. "I plan to do a special piece on Bob Dale for the magazine. You're my best source about what really happened."

"He was beaten to death by a person or persons unknown—so far," Peter said. "There are so many people crowded into his life that it may take forever to sort them out and write them off." Peter took a sip of his drink. "You know an actor named Lucien Smallwood, Max?"

"Oh, God, that clown!" Lewis said. He took the handkerchief out of his sleeve and touched his lips with it, as though he were wiping away a bad taste.

"I understand Gavin Hayes fired him after a day of rehearsals for *Triangle.*"

"He is a very fat man with a voice like a foghorn," Lewis said. "Every now and then somebody hires him because the physical monstrosity that he is seems to fit some outsized part. The poor bastard can't act his way out of a paper bag, however. He was blackballed when somebody put him up for membership here at The Players because he is a jerk, not because he can't act. He's a genius at the art of how-not-to-make-it."

"I understand he thought Dale was responsible for getting him fired this time," Peter said.

"Bob Dale was a real pro," Lewis said. "He couldn't bear to work with phonies. Maybe he did get him fired. As the star of the show he would have had the clout."

"You know where Smallwood can be located?"

Lewis shrugged. "Probably some cheap Broadway fleabag or cold-water flat. Actors Equity probably has an address for him. He hangs around there, studying the notices for open auditions on the call-board."

"Gavin Hayes must have an address for him," Peter said. "Incidently, Max, if you want background on Dale, Sam Cowley is your man." He gestured toward the table where the rabbit-faced octogenarian was holding forth to a restive audience.

"That old creep!" Lewis said. "I have a special favor to ask of you, Peter."

"If you want to talk about the case, Max, give me a breather until tomorrow. I'm just about dead of it."

The sardonic Lewis smile moved the critic's lips. "There's talk around that you were meant to be dead of it, chum; that the killer didn't know you'd rented your apartment to Dale."

"Which will not contribute to sound sleeping," Peter said.

"Don't tell me you're going back to your apartment?"

"Where else?" Peter said. "It's got to be faced sometime."

"But this killer knows his way in—apparently could accomplish it so noiselessly that he didn't wake Dale. Wild horses couldn't drag me there until that monster is caught!" Lewis said. "I mean, if I were you."

Peter drank and put the empty glass down on the bar. "If someone's after me I wish he'd come and we'd get it over with," he said. "Thanks for the drink, Max."

"Aren't you afraid?"

"Sure, I'm afraid," Peter said. "Only a dummy without imagination isn't afraid when he's threatened." He gave Lewis a thin smile. "Are you interviewing me for your piece on Bob Dale, Max?"

"No, no," Lewis said. "I operate by Devery's Law. Always give due warning when an interview begins, like a cop

62

reading a prisoner his rights. The favor I wanted to ask is something else."

"So ask," Peter said.

"Just between you and me," Lewis said, "I've written a play."

"Congratulations," Peter said. "Surely you're not going to ask me to read it, Max. The theater isn't my ballpark."

"No," Lewis said, "though I'd be flattered if you wanted to. It's something quite different. You see, I gave a copy of it to Bob Dale to read. That was just a couple of days ago. He hadn't gotten back to me about it; perhaps he hadn't had a chance to read it."

"Surely it wasn't the only copy," Peter said.

"My top copy," Lewis said. "Notes, inserts, editings. Dale himself may have made notes. I asked him to. That particular copy is invaluable. I have to assume it's in your apartment."

"If it is I couldn't give it to you," Peter said, "Maxvil's coming in the morning to collect all of Dale's belongings. Until he does they are, in effect, impounded."

Lewis laughed. "I wasn't planning to work on it to-night," he said. "But I'd feel better if I knew it was there and safe; that Bob hadn't left it on a subway or in a taxi."

"I'll take a look for it," Peter said. "I have to tell you I was there most of the day and didn't see it lying around." He shook his head. "A play by Max Lewis, the critic, isn't something I'd be likely to forget about. That's news, Max."

"I hope you won't make it news," Lewis said. "Not until something positive happens about it. There is a marvelous part in it which I hoped Bob Dale couldn't resist. That's why I gave it to him to read. Would you mind if I walked back with you, just to reassure myself?"

"Max, I'm dead for sleep."

"Hell, Peter, it's only two rooms. Bob wouldn't have

63

hidden it under a floorboard or buried it in the garden. It would only take a few minutes to have a look."

"It could be in his dressing room at the Boswell Theater," Peter said. He didn't want Lewis's company. He wanted to be by himself.

"The house manager at the theater checked out Bob's dressing room for me," Lewis said. "It isn't there."

Peter sighed. "So come along," he said.

For all his distaste for Lewis, Peter found he was grateful for his company as they walked to Irving Place. The Maxvil-Devery theory had really gotten to him. Perhaps it was because he was too damned tired to contemplate facing an emergency alone.

The police had left the apartment looking almost too orderly. It didn't feel normal. Peter wondered if it ever would again. Peter and Lewis did a quick search of the living room, in Peter's desk, in the bookcases where the play-script might have been put down. Lewis was like a bird dog, trying to pick up a scent. He headed for the bedroom, pausing in the doorway.

"This where it happened?" he asked.

Peter nodded. "I don't imagine Dale took your play to bed with him," he said.

"Reading in bed is not an uncommon practice," Lewis said. He went over to the bed, opened the drawers of the bedside table. No script. "Mind if I look in the bureau, Peter?"

He didn't wait for an answer. Peter felt a slow anger beginning to rise in him.

"Are you by any chance violating Devery's Law?" he asked.

Lewis's sardonic smile reappeared. "I suppose I am, Peter. The scene of the crime will fit into my piece on Dale. So, due warning."

Lewis walked back into the living room, opened the French doors, and stepped out into the garden. "The killer came this way?" he asked.

"They assume," Peter said. He'd had it. "Your script isn't here, Max. I'd appreciate it if you'd take off and let me hit the sack. If you want to gather color for your piece, come back tomorrow, or some other time."

"No hard feelings," Lewis said. He came back into the living room and closed the French doors. "If I were you I'd prop a couple of chairs against these doors so you'd surely hear someone trying to break in. And if you come across the script—"

"Is there really a script, Max?" Peter asked.

Lewis laughed. "My dear fellow, of course there is, and Bob has left it somewhere. I'd say 'sleep well,' but I don't suppose you can."

The front door closed on Lewis, and Peter was alone. Nosy bastard, Peter thought. There are minds for whom a direct approach is impossible. If Lewis had wanted to visit "the scene of the crime" to give color to his special article, he could have asked, simply and directly, and Peter, working for the same magazine, would have made it possible—as a favor to Devery, if not to Lewis. The absurd invention of a missing manuscript indicated how deviously Lewis had to approach things, or perhaps how certain he was that Peter wouldn't do him a simple favor.

In the end Peter found he couldn't face the business of making up the bed with clean sheets. He didn't undress, but lay down on the couch in the living room after bracing two chairs from the kitchenette against the French doors. Damn Lewis for rearousing his anxiety.

He was tired enough for sleep to come almost instantly. It was some hours later that he found himself off the couch and crouching in the middle of the room. Something had waked him out of a deep, dark oblivion.

It was the telephone, ringing stubbornly in the bedroom.

Early dawn light was seeping through the glass of the French doors. Peter walked a little unsteadily into the bedroom. The electric clock on the bedside table showed him that it was a few minutes before five. He had slept for just three hours.

"Peter?" It was Maxvil.

"You calling to find out if I was asleep?" Peter asked, annoyed.

"We're involved with a daisy chain," Maxvil said.

"Speak English, will you, Greg!"

"The night watchman at the Boswell Theater has just reported finding Gavin Hayes shot to death in his office there." Maxvil's voice was matter-of-fact, as though he were reporting on the weather. That casual voice, Peter knew, disguised anger and tension.

"Not real!" Peter said.

"Shot while he was sitting at his desk. The medical examiner is on his way so I can't tell you yet when it happened. I'm just headed there myself. Can I pick you up on the way?"

"You think there's a connection—?"

"It has," Maxvil said with sudden bitterness, "occurred to me!"

PART TWO

1

The Boswell Theater is just west of Broadway in the mid-forties. It, too, is a kind of landmark in the theater district. It was here that Jonathan Boswell, the legendary impresario, had staged so many great successes around the turn of the century and into the golden age of the twenties. It was from its roof that Jonathan Boswell had taken a swan dive after the stock-market crash of twenty-nine. The theater, known in those days as the Markham, was mortgaged to the hilt. It was bought by some up-and-coming young man who had foreseen the crash and kept his money; he renamed it for the dead maestro and refurbished it, and then it had gone on for the next fifty years as a much sought-after house for small-cast, intimate plays like *Triangle*. At night, with the lights of Broadway all around it, it nestled comfortably, with a kind of old-world glamour. The marquee was held up by two stone gargoyles with the comic and tragic theater masks for faces, carved by some forgotten nineteenth-century sculptor. The interior, with its dark reds and gold trim, when softly lighted for an incoming audience, was warm and inviting, promising the delights of theatrical magic.

At five thirty in the morning it looked old and defeated to Peter. The light bulbs in the marquee spelling out ROBERT DALE in TRIANGLE looked dirty and unused. Bits of paper and other trash blew around outside the closed lobby doors. Inside, Peter knew, it was a place of death, not of magic.

Peter and Maxvil had ridden uptown in a police car, driven by a uniformed patrolman. Maxvil was in a dark, angry mood.

"Sometimes I get so sick of this stinking business," he said to Peter. "It's always after the fact. We never seem to prevent anything. Goddamn it, Peter, was there anything in our conversations with Gavin Hayes that made you think he was in any kind of danger?"

"Nothing."

"I had him down for a prime suspect."

"I know. I didn't think so. After talking to Deborah Wallace I was sure he wasn't. The two crimes don't have to have any connection, Greg. Hayes had a very active life in the business, much of it that had nothing whatever to do with Bob Dale."

"Well, I'm stuck with it," Maxvil said. "Someone else would normally cover this territory, but the Commissioner believes the murders tie in together."

"Just because both men were involved in this play, producer and star?"

"You can't ignore that," Maxvil said. "Both of them killed within twenty-four hours of each other. Well, we'll see. Maybe we'll see."

There had been no chance to brief Maxvil on his visit with Deborah Wallace, and Peter suddenly realized that the detective knew nothing about the actor Lucien Smallwood, who had been objected to by Dale and fired by Hayes. Max Lewis had not drawn a pretty picture of Smallwood. It

70

wasn't impossible that this embittered failure—a "genius at how-not-to-make-it," Lewis had called him—was out to get revenge for his firing.

"Max Lewis suggested Hayes would know where to locate him," Peter said.

"But Hayes isn't talking," Maxvil said.

"Actors Equity, when they open up this morning."

"By then Master Smallwood, if he is our man, could be in Mexico!" Maxvil said.

A uniformed cop was standing inside the lobby doors of the Boswell, shielded from the swirling dust and debris on the sidewalk. He opened one of the doors to let Peter and Maxvil in. The lobby was still decorated with pictures from *Triangle* of Dale, Deborah Wallace, and other members of the cast.

"The office is way up on the fifth floor, Lieutenant," the cop said. "There's an elevator—but it doesn't work."

"Oh, joy!" Maxvil said.

"Sergeant Burke is up there, sir. The medical examiner's crew still haven't arrived. The stairway goes up from backstage. A man there will show you where it is."

A garish work light hung over the center of the stage, giving the empty theater a bleak, cold look. The set for *Triangle*—a modern living room—was still in place, dust sheets covering the furniture. Another uniformed cop was standing at the back of the stage.

"Up here, Lieutenant," he called out. His voice echoed slightly in the empty theater.

They walked down the side aisle and up four steps in front of the right-hand stage box.

"There's an elevator," the officer said, "but—"

"—it doesn't work," Maxvil said.

An iron stairway going up in a leisurely circle took them past the actors' dressing rooms, a costume shop, a storage area for electrical equipment. Looking out over the ropes, pulleys, and weights above the stage Peter saw a scene dock at the rear of the theater.

The fifth floor was something else again. It was enclosed, shut off from the stage and the theater. The hallway was thickly carpeted. A couple of small offices opened off it, their doors standing open. At the end of the hall was a large oak door with heavy, wrought-iron hinges. On the door was a name in gold letters, JONATHAN BOSWELL. The famous old impresario was fifty years dead but not forgotten.

Sergeant Burke was standing just inside the door of the office. The room itself caught Peter's attention almost before he took in the bloody disaster at the carved, Florentine desk. It was a huge room with an almost cathedral-like high ceiling. A large skylight with diamond-shaped panes of glass let in the first beams of the morning light. Those beams of light, like some carefully planned staging, shone directly down on what was left of Gavin Hayes. The Oriental rug that covered the floor from wall to wall was, Peter knew, probably priceless.

Peter forced himself to look at Gavin Hayes.

Hayes had obviously been working at his desk when he was confronted by someone with a gun. A seersucker jacket was hung over the back of the chair in which he was sitting. He had fallen forward, his left cheek resting on some papers or reports he'd been working on. His right hand was stretched forward, as if he'd been reaching in death for a pack of cigarettes and a lighter that were just out of reach. Blood covered the whole top surface of the desk. The side of Hayes's face that was visible had a small wound at the temple.

"Exit wound," Burke was explaining to Maxvil. "Bullet's over there in the paneling. I didn't want to dig it out till you got here, Lieutenant. I didn't want to touch him till the

M.E. got here, but Mr. McNamara lifted him up for a moment.''

"You could drive a truck through that side of his head," a husky voice said from a dark corner of the room.

For the first time Peter noticed a man standing in the shadows, backed away as far as the wall would let him go.

Pat McNamara, a grizzled Irishman, had been the night watchman at the Boswell Theater for thirty years. Included in his responsibilities were two other theaters down the block. He made the rounds, covering each of the three theaters four or five times in the night. The Boswell had not been designed for the convenience of a watchman. The five flights of dressing rooms and offices were hell to cover without the elevator working.

On this last night the theater had been dark, no performance because of the death of Robert Dale. McNamara had satisfied himself about the stage and lower dressing-room areas. No reason for anyone to be in the upper offices. The box office in the lobby had stayed open until nine o'clock to deal with customers who had somehow missed the news of Dale's death and come to see a performance that would never be given, and others who had heard and wanted refunds or tickets for future performances. After nine o'clock the Boswell was deserted.

McNamara, finding the elevator out of order, had simply not gone to the upper floors. But about four, or a little after, while it was still dark, he had come back from one of his other theaters and stopped across the street at an all-night lunchroom for a cup of coffee. Coming out he glanced up and saw lights in the windows of Jonathan Boswell's office—Hayes's office these days. He was sure they hadn't been on earlier, and so he re-entered the theater and climbed the endless iron stairway to the top.

"He was just like he is now," McNamara said. "I didn't stop to think, and I lifted him up a few inches. When I saw there was nothing left of that side of his head I eased him back down again and called the cops."

"No sign of anyone else in the theater?" Maxvil said.

"I scrammed out of here," McNamara said. "After I called the cops."

"Using that phone on the desk?"

"Yes, sir. I ran around hollering for someone. I—I didn't want to be alone with him." He nodded toward the body. "There wasn't anybody. I ran out on the street, looking for a cop. But like always, there's never one around when you need one."

"They can't be everywhere at once, Mr. McNamara," Maxvil said cheerfully. "We'd have to have a cop for every non-cop in the city to manage that."

"I'm sorry," McNamara said. "I guess it's just something people say."

"Did Mr. Hayes often work here late at night?" Maxvil said.

"No. Maybe till an hour after the curtain. Usually not working, but he'd have people up here for a drink. People always want to see the great Boswell's office. That cabinet over there has an ice maker in it and a supply of booze. Sometimes he'd go around the corner to Sardi's. But he had headaches tonight, I imagine; Bob Dale dead and the show closed. Big advance he'd have to refund. You could guess some of that advance money had already gone into expenses. To tell you the truth, Lieutenant, I figure he must have come back here very late. When the box-office people closed up around nine I asked them if there was anyone in the offices—knowing the elevator was on the fritz. They said everyone was long gone—drowning their sorrows, they said."

74

"You don't remember looking up from the street earlier and not seeing the light?"

"I certainly didn't look up before that and see it," McNamara said. "I'd of checked then if I had."

"How would Hayes get into the theater after everyone had gone?" Maxvil asked.

"Hell, Lieutenant, he was leasing the theater. It was like he owned it. He had keys to the stage-door entrance, to this office. He could come and go whenever."

"So he comes back here late to work. How could somebody else get in, because somebody did?"

McNamara looked unhappy. "Three ways," he said, slowly. "Of course he could have come in with Mr. Hayes."

"Hayes was obviously working at figures," Maxvil said. "Would he be doing that if he brought a guest in with him?"

"Somebody could have phoned him and he went downstairs and let him in," McNamara said.

"And the third way?"

"The theater was open all day," McNamara said. "Cops asking questions, actors and stagehands and others coming to collect their belongings. The show was closed. Box-office people here all day."

"You're saying someone could have come in early and hidden in the theater?"

"Could be."

"But you checked it out several times during the evening."

"Jesus, Lieutenant, I didn't look in every closet and behind every drape. My job is to check for fire—some jerk leaving a butt burning somewhere, or any kind of vandalism. And I didn't go upstairs on account of the elevator being out. I'm not a kid anymore, Lieutenant, and those stairs are tough. I was sure there was no one up there."

"But there could have been?"

"I suppose."

Specialists from Homicide and the medical examiner's office all seemed to arrive at once. They worked with a kind of brisk efficiency that Peter had seen before and which never ceased to amaze him. There were fewer uncertainties about Hayes's murder than there had been yesterday in the Dale case. There were no doubts about the weapon used. The bullet dug out of the paneling and the wound determined that it had been a heavy-type handgun, probably a .44-caliber weapon. There was no question about the way the murderer had come to the fifth-floor office. The elevator had been out of service since the day before, it was determined. It was a vintage mechanism, and the repair people had to make the replacement parts needed. The murderer could only have come up the winding, iron stair from the stage area, by invitation or by stealth. Or it could have been someone whose comings and goings would have been normal, unnoticed. Like, Peter thought, a night watchman. He wondered, as he watched the fingerprint men and the police photographer at work, what Gavin Hayes's relationship with old Pat McNamara had been? Old-timers, like McNamara, become very possessive about properties with which they're involved. For thirty years McNamara had been responsible for the Boswell's security. In that time there must have been a hundred different tenants like Gavin Hayes, leasing the theater from the owners for the run of a play. McNamara would have his own, unvarying routines. If a temporary tenant tried to interfere with them, that could start flaming resentments.

It was a far-out notion, but Peter found he couldn't shake it. The old man had been taken to an adjoining office, which, Peter learned, was used by the stage manager, to

76

make a formal statement to a police stenographer under Sergeant Burke's questioning. The medical examiner's men were preparing to remove Gavin Hayes's body, and that was an operation Peter didn't care to watch. A dead body is handled so impersonally, so without feeling by the professionals. Peter wandered out into the hall to wait for Pat McNamara to finish making his statement. He could hear the old man talking into a tape machine, retelling the same story he'd told Maxvil, almost word for word. Finally McNamara came out into the hall, wiping at his unshaven face with a red bandana handkerchief.

"They ask you the same questions so many times it almost drives you nuts," he said to Peter.

"I guess they want to make sure you haven't left anything out," Peter said. "Can I ask you a couple of questions off the record, Pat?"

"How come they have a reporter working with the cops?" McNamara asked.

"Robert Dale was murdered in my apartment," Peter said. "The lieutenant's an old friend of mine. I guess he thinks I might be helpful. There's a chance there's a connection between the two murders."

"I feel real bad about Mr. Dale," McNamara said. "A real nice guy. He made friends with everyone—stagehands, box-office people, even the ushers and the house people. He found out I had two grandchildren and he bought them one of those mechano-building sets. I've seen a hell of a lot of stars come and go in this theater. He was just about the most decent one of the whole lot."

"You didn't feel as warmly about Gavin Hayes?"

McNamara shrugged. "Hardly knew him."

"But you worked for him."

"Not me! Maybe you don't understand how a theater like this works, Mr. Styles. The box-office people, the house manager, the ushers, and me, for instance, work for the owner. A producer—like Mr. Hayes—leases the theater from the owner. He brings in his actors and his backstage people, but the regular staff works for the owner."

"Who is—?"

"Jake Goldman," McNamara said. He looked surprised when the name didn't seem to register with Peter. "Jake's grandfather bought this theater after old man Boswell jumped off the roof in twenty-nine. Bought a half-a-dozen other theaters, too, at that time. Good real-estate buy, and the original Jake Goldman was a shrewd operator. His sons took over from him when he died, and Marty Goldman was the present Jake's father. Today's Jake owns and operates maybe ten theaters, including the two others I cover in this block. I've worked for the Goldmans, one or the other of them, for thirty-five years, maintenance man at first, then watchman after arthritis set in and I couldn't handle tools."

"So you had no dealings with Gavin Hayes?"

McNamara's smile was thin. "I think he spoke to me once, the first night his company was in the theater. He saw me backstage and asked, 'Who the hell are you?' I told him I was the night watchman. Only words he ever spoke to me. After that he'd walk by me as though I wasn't there."

"You carry a gun on the job, Pat?" Peter asked.

McNamara chuckled. "Sergeant Burke asked me that. I guess he figured I might have a reason for knocking off Hayes."

"Did you?"

"I was a zero to him and he was a zero to me," McNamara said. "Mr. Dale was something else again. A real nice guy, thoughtful of everyone."

Except, Peter thought, one Lucien Smallwood.

"I used to carry a gun in the old days," McNamara said. "I couldn't of shot anyone with it, but it was a threat. But

78

you don't get anywhere threatening today's crooks. They shoot you dead before you can open your mouth. Today if I find anyone in one of my theaters who hadn't ought to be there, I head for the alarm box that calls the protective agency guys. Show a gun and you've had it.''

Maxvil was not a man to wait for other people's routines to work out. He located someone who worked in Actors Equity's offices and had him go there early to find an address for Lucien Smallwood. Some fleabag hotel Max Lewis had suggested, and that's just what it turned out to be. Some fifty years ago the Greystone may have been a luxury hotel; now it was a housing disaster. Most of it was occupied by Welfare cases, and its hallways were littered. The desk clerk, unshaven, shirt-sleeved, and red-eyed from some kind of overnight celebrating, wasn't civil, even when Maxvil showed his police badge.

"Smallwood's in three-sixteen," the clerk said. "And you can tell that drunken sonofabitch for me that if he doesn't settle his bill by noon today he's out on his butt!"

There was a self-service elevator that Maxvil and Peter almost hesitated to use. It wheezed and groaned as it lifted them, jerkily, to the third floor. Maxvil knocked firmly on the door of three-sixteen.

"Go away!" a thick but powerful voice shouted at them from the inside.

"It's the police, Mr. Smallwood," Maxvil said.

"Don't play games with me, you wall-eyed bastard!" Smallwood yelled. "I'll pay up when I'm good and goddamn ready!"

"I am the police, not the clerk, Mr. Smallwood," Maxvil said.

Perhaps the man inside, half-awake, recognized the voice of authority. "Hold the fort!" he called out.

The door opened after a moment or two, and Peter found himself stepping back. The man who filled the doorway was a giant, almost six and a half feet tall and weighing a good three hundred pounds. He was wearing slacks and a dirty white shirt. He was barefoot, his feet dirty. He had a heavy black beard and his little black shoe-button eyes were red-rimmed. His breath was overpowering, even from a few feet away, with the sick, stale smell of cheap whiskey. He squinted at Maxvil's shield in its leather case.

"They don't call the cops to collect the rent," he boomed at them. "So what the hell do you want? I could show you plenty of work for the police in this dump!"

"Gavin Hayes was shot to death in his office at the Boswell Theater early this morning," Maxvil said. "I imagine you can understand why I want to talk to you about it."

"Oh, brother," the giant said. "Sonofabitch had it coming to him. So come in, Lieutenant, if you don't mind talking in a garbage heap."

It was an apt description. The room was almost too small to house a man of Smallwood's size. It was littered with empty beer cans, brown paper bags, pieces of wax paper that had once wrapped sandwiches. A door stood open to a tiny bathroom, and the odor from it was unpleasant. There was a rumpled bed that looked as if there hadn't been clean sheets on it for weeks. One window opened onto the brick of an adjoining building not six feet away. Scarcely any air or light came through. There was one straight-backed chair over which a suit jacket was hung. Resting in front of it was a pair of shoes, the size of small boats, and a pair of Argyle socks.

"I'd suggest sitting down if there was any place to sit," Smallwood said. "Jesus! I just got through celebrating one murder and you bring me news of another! How do you like that?"

"I don't like it, Mr. Smallwood. That's why I'm here." Maxvil said. "This is Peter Styles of *Newsview Magazine*."

"The press!" Smallwood said. "An interview, no less! Be sure you spell my name right, Mr. Styles. It's L-u-c-i-e-n—e-n, not a-n."

"I'll make an effort," Peter said.

"Shot, you say? In his office?" Smallwood was searching for something in his trouser pockets. "I think I smoked my last butt. Do either of you—?"

Maxvil handed him his pack of Camels. Smallwood's huge hands shook as he extracted one. He tried lighting a kitchen match with his thumbnail and couldn't make it. Peter held out his lighter. The three of them made a crowd in the tiny room.

"You had a quarrel with Hayes and he fired you," Maxvil said. "I understand you've been shouting threats all over town. Robert Dale is another one you announced you would eliminate."

"My two best friends!" Smallwood said. His laughter shook the open window in its frame. "How often does a man find someone else to pay off his debts?"

"What were your troubles with Dale and Hayes?" Maxvil asked.

The big man sat down on the edge of the bed. He took a deep drag on his cigarette, choked, coughed. "You can imagine," he said, gasping for breath, "that I have some difficulty finding jobs for myself as an actor. Oh, things were going pretty well a few years back—in Hollywood. I played tough guys, and monsters, and men from outer space. I thought I had a chance to play the Incredible Hulk in a TV series, but someone else got it. Then I—I put the slug on some TV producer and I found myself blacklisted. Oh, they won't admit there is any such thing as a blacklist, but if you can't get work, what else is it?"

"You knew Dale and Hayes out there?"

"I didn't know Dale, but I was in a film with him—an extra bit. Heard of Hayes, but I never met him or worked with him. So when Hollywood dried up I came looking for work here. Not much chance of a Broadway show, being what I am, but there was a chance for TV commercials and industrial films. No luck, though. I wound up here. Then I got my big break. They were casting for *Triangle,* and the script called for a professional wrestler—a really great comedy part. You see the show?"

Neither Maxvil nor Peter had.

"Best chance I ever had on Broadway, and I got it. Well, I celebrated for a couple of days and went to the first rehearsal. I guess I was not only hung over, I was still a little potted. Dale blew his stack. Everybody said he was a decent guy and I begged him for another chance. He wouldn't give an inch. He wouldn't work with an alcoholic, he said. Better to end it then than later, when we were well into production. I swore on my mother's grave I wouldn't take another drink for the run of the play. He wouldn't listen. Decent guy, my foot! Hayes stood with him and fired me. Sure, I stormed around town threatening to cut off their balls. But of course I didn't."

"Did you know where Dale was living?"

"Yesterday—I read in the paper he was in Mr. Styles's apartment."

"I think I have to ask you to account for your movements in the last thirty-six hours," Maxvil said.

Smallwood dropped his cigarette on the floor, and stomped it out with his bare foot. He seemed not to feel any pain.

"I was drunk, somewhere," he said. "Someone told me Dale was dead. I really poured it on then, and the next thing I remember is—is you knocking on my door here."

"That won't do," Maxvil said. "Just go back over it and try to remember where you were, who you were with."

The little black eyes focused on the detective. "I have just one reason for drinking, Lieutenant. It's to blot out the whole disgusting world. I don't want to remember where I am or who I'm with. I manage to accomplish that most of the time. I suppose if an elephant wanders in the jungle, he leaves his spoor. I must have done enough unmentionable things in the last thirty-six hours to leave a trail. But I'm telling you the truth, Lieutenant. I don't know where to begin to look."

"But you didn't kill Dale or Hayes?"

Smallwood's thunderous laugh was jarring. "I suppose I could. God knows I had reason!"

"Do you own a .44-caliber handgun?" Maxvil asked.

"I don't own anything of any value," Smallwood said. "Anything I ever did own, including the fillings in my teeth, are in a hockshop somewhere. There has to be some way to pay for my oblivion."

Watching Maxvil, Peter guessed that the detective believed Smallwood's story of a blackout. The man's miserable condition, the humiliating surroundings, were enough to account for his wanting to erase each living moment from his memory.

"And you have no clue as to where you were early this morning and early yesterday morning?" Maxvil asked.

"Not a clue—God help me." Smallwood gave Maxvil a strange, twisted little smile. "If I did kill them, it would solve all my problems, wouldn't it? I mean, I wouldn't have to worry about what tomorrow holds for me, would I?"

"You're talking like a self-indulgent child, Mr. Smallwood," Maxvil said. "Don't worry, we'll pick up your 'spoor,' as you put it. You could help by telling me what some of your regular haunts are."

"I don't have any regular haunts anymore, Lieutenant," Smallwood said. "I walk in some place I'm known and I get kicked out on my ass before I can ask for a glass of water. I've started too many fights, broken too much glassware, smashed too many mirrors to be welcome anyplace I'm known."

"Places in this neighborhood?"

"Ran out of them long ago," Smallwood said.

"It doesn't bother you that you may have killed two men during one of your blackouts?"

"It would be better to find out I'd killed those two men than some innocent bystander. At least I had a reason to want those two bastards dead!"

2

The carbon-monoxide-filled air on the street outside the Greystone Hotel seemed like a blessed relief to Peter after those few minutes in Lucien Smallwood's evil-smelling hole.

"How does a man let himself fall into such a situation?" he said to Maxvil.

The detective shrugged. "If I had time I'd feel sorry for him," he said.

"You think he really doesn't know?"

" 'You pays your money and you takes your choice,' " Maxvil said. "A guilty man usually denies his guilt. That one almost hopes he may have done it. It would solve his unsolvable problems. But we've got to prove him out, one way or the other. It shouldn't be too hard. A runaway locomotive like that can't go unnoticed. Nobody would ever forget seeing him. My God, he's big!"

"But he does have a connection with both the dead men," Peter said.

"So do dozens of other people in the theater and movie world," Maxvil said. He threw a half-smoked cigarette into the gutter. "We're not just looking for a needle in a haystack. We're looking for a specific needle in a haystack full of needles, for God's sake."

Peter knew what Maxvil was facing; without any real lead he was confronted with a long, grueling search among hundreds of friends and acquaintances of the two dead men. He might be looking for one murderer or two. The two murders might be connected or they might not be. Maxvil's investigation had to consider both possibilities.

"A great time for a vacation in Tahiti," Maxvil said.

"I'm thinking about Deborah Wallace," Peter said. "The two men who have played the biggest roles in her life both dead within a day."

"In shock, no doubt," Maxvil said.

"If she knows."

Maxvil shrugged. "Radio and TV." He lit a fresh cigarette. "You think you made friends with her?"

"I think so."

"Will you take one more shot at it? Surround her with cops, tape machines, stenographers, and she may come unglued. If you can ease her through an informal beginning, she may be our very best source of help. Both Dale and Hayes were in positions to talk more intimately to her about their lives than to anyone else. I've got to get the final word from the medical examiner. After that, the lady's going to have to talk to me, to someone from the district attorney's office, the whole *schmear*. If you can get her ready for it—?"

"I'll try," Peter said.

He went to a pay phone in a corner drugstore and dialed Deborah's number. She answered on the second ring.

"My God, Peter, I've been trying to reach you for the last couple of hours—more!"

"You know?" he said.

"The house manager at the Boswell called me," she said "You—saw him?"

"Gavin? Yes. He never knew what hit him, Deborah. Listen, you're going to be swarmed over by cops, prosecutors, and God knows who else in a little while. Can I talk to you first?"

"Please, Peter! I'm so frightened."

"Frightened of what? The Homicide man in charge of the case is a friend of mine, a very decent and considerate guy."

"It's not that, Peter! About an hour ago my phone rang. I thought it might be Tony Hutton, the house manager, calling back with something new about Gavin. Nobody spoke when I answered—but there was someone there, Peter. I could hear—hear breathing. A breather! Like out of an old B movie."

"Sit tight," Peter said. "I'll be right along—ten minutes."

"That isn't all, Peter. About ten minutes ago someone knocked on my door. No one had rung the front-door bell, I hadn't released the front-door lock. He kept knocking—and saying in a low voice—'This is the building inspector, Miss Wallace.' There wouldn't be any building inspector without the superintendent being with him. Someone was trying to persuade me to let them in. I—I've called the police!"

"Good girl," Peter said. "Don't let anyone in but cops, and be sure they're cops. A cab should get me there in a hurry."

"Oh, Peter!"

Out on the street Maxvil was long gone. Peter flagged down a cab, and the driver took Peter at his word about urgency. He cut east to Park Avenue, south as fast as the lights would let him, around the ramp at Grand Central, and east on Thirty-eighth Street. A police patrol car was standing outside Deborah's building. At least the cops had responded promptly. Peter paid off his driver, adding a generous tip, and rang the bell under Deborah's name in the vestibule. A man's voice came over the intercom.

"Who is it?"

"Peter Styles. Miss Wallace is expecting me."

There was a moment's hesitation and then the door lock clicked and Peter let himself in. A uniformed patrolman stood at the top of the inner stairway, brighter by daylight than it had been the night before.

"You got some kind of I.D.?" the cop asked as Peter reached the second floor.

Peter produced his wallet with his driver's license and credit and press cards. "Miss Wallace can identify me," he said. "Is she all right?"

"Scared but OK," the cop said.

Deborah came out into the hall and ran straight into Peter's arms, crying softly. "Oh Peter, Peter!"

He held her gently for a moment and then eased her back into the apartment.

"It might be a good idea if you'd try to reach Lieutenant Maxvil of Homicide," he said over his shoulder to the cop. "He's probably at the medical examiner's office. This is a little more complex than it might appear on the surface."

"I'm Murphy, Fifteenth Precinct," the cop said. "The lady has explained a little."

Peter sat down on the couch with Deborah, his arm around her. She buried her face on his shoulder, still crying.

"Somebody rang the bell for a tenant on the third floor," Murphy said, "She thought it was her cleaning woman and released the front-door lock without trying to identify the caller over the intercom. When the cleaning woman didn't arrive she went out onto the landing and called down. A man's voice said he was sorry, he'd rung the wrong bell. So

88

the lady just went back into her apartment and forgot about it till we questioned her. My partner's searching the building. Use your phone, Miss Wallace? I'd like to locate Lieutenant Maxvil."

Deborah nodded, clinging to Peter.

The primary questions were who and why? "Connection" was a word they had been throwing around for the last twenty-four hours and more. Was there any connection between the murders of Bob Dale and Gavin Hayes? Now Peter was asking himself if there was any connection between the murders and this curious attempt to get at Deborah Wallace?

"Has anything like this ever happened to you before, Deborah?" he asked her. "This 'breather' on the telephone?"

She shook her head, still out of control.

"The woods are full of kooks like that," Murphy said. "We get half-a-dozen complaints a week at the Precinct. Girls and young women living alone. Some pervert spots 'em on the street, follows 'em home, gets their names somehow, calls on the phone. It's like they're having a sexual experience. Later, maybe, they try to get to them— like this one tried. You notice anyone following you around out in the neighborhood, Miss Wallace?"

Again the shake of the head. Her fingernails were biting into Peter's arm.

"Take it easy, luv," Peter said. "You're perfectly safe. Nobody's going to get to you."

"Tomorrow? The next day?" She choked the words out.

"You'll be protected as long as it's necessary, Miss Wallace," Murphy said. He went to the phone. He evidently had emergency numbers in his notebook. A moment or two later he had Maxvil on the phone and gave him a rundown. "It's some pervert, Lieutenant. We get complaints all the time. But Mr. Styles thought—" He turned to Peter. "The Lieutenant would like to talk to you."

Maxvil sounded cool and efficient. "The lady badly shaken up?" he asked.

"Yes."

"We're asking ourselves the same question, I imagine."

"Yes."

"I'm on my way," Maxvil said.

There was a knock on the door and Deborah cried out.

"Easy, Miss Wallace," Murphy said. "It's my partner."

Patrolman Kosufski, a stocky blond, had been over the house from cellar to roof. He had been into each of the eight apartments in the building.

"He's long gone," Kosufski said. "Probably heard Miss Wallace dialing the phone when he was outside the door. No one saw him. No one had any reason to be looking for him. The lady in Three-B heard him speak. That's it."

"Maybe we should have a look around the block," Murphy said. "He could be hanging around, waiting for us to take off."

"You stay here," Kosufski said. "I'll have a look around. You have no idea who he could be, what he might look like, Miss Wallace?"

"No, no, no!" Deborah said, clinging to Peter, who had come back from the phone.

"Glamorous actress," Kosufski said. "Just the kind of woman these perverts would have an eye for."

"It isn't that!" Deborah said. She took a deep, sobbing breath that seemed to help her gain control. "Don't you see, Peter? *Triangle!* We were all connected with *Triangle.*"

A husband, a wife, a lover—the classic triangle, Peter thought.

90

"I don't get it," Kosufski said.

"Two murders and this," Peter said. "Miss Wallace, Robert Dale, and Gavin Hayes were all involved in a Broadway play called *Triangle*."

"That maniac, Smallwood!" Deborah said.

"No chance, luv," Peter said. "Maxvil and I were with Smallwood when this was happening to you. Whatever else he may have done he didn't phone you or knock on your door."

"He hired somebody to come after me," Deborah said, hysteria close.

"He doesn't have the money to ride a crosstown bus," Peter said. "Smallwood wasn't here, Deborah."

"Oh my God!" she said. "Then who, Peter? Someone connected with the play. It must be, don't you see?"

These three people had been intertwined in one way or another for fifteen years, Peter thought. They were a triangle, but it need not have anything to do with the play *Triangle*.

"I'll scout around outside," Kosufski said, and went away. He was still riding the pervert theory.

Peter had no theory that held water. Someone involved with the play, someone they hadn't even thought of up to now.

"You say the house manager called you to tell you about Gavin?" he asked Deborah.

She nodded. "Tony Hutton. I think someone called the theater owner to tell him about—about Gavin, and Mr. Goldman, the owner, got in touch with Tony. Tony knew I was still married to Gavin—"

"Was there trouble in the company, Deborah?"

"No. Everyone seemed to get along fine—except for Smallwood that first day of rehearsals. Smooth as glass.

Gavin directed, you know. No problems with anyone after Smallwood. Gavin and Bob were great to work with, kept everyone happy.''

"You encounter a night watchman named McNamara?"

"Oh, yes. He found Gavin, didn't he?"

"Yes."

"A nice old man. Bob liked him. I actually went with Bob to buy some toys for his grandchildren.''

"All sweetness and light in the company, then?"

"It was a small cast, Peter. Bob and me, Sandra Lake, the ingenue, Eddie Marks, the juvenile, and Joe Becket, who took over the part of the wrestler that Smallwood was originally hired for. We all worked well together. No tensions at all.''

"What about the house people, the regular staff?"

"Tony Hutton, a nice guy, married, kids. Bert Brown, the box-office treasurer is an old-timer who's worked for the Goldmans for years and years. There's a young man and a girl who work with Bert—I just know them as Paul and Betty.''

"Stagehands?"

"There are four or five of them, but I don't really know them,'' Deborah said. "There's no set change in the play, but the union requires you hire stagehands anyway. They spend most of their time playing cards in the basement or watching TV.''

"That's it?"

"Oh, there's Lou Nason, the stage manager. Marvelous at his job. Never a slip up of any kind. Bob used to say that Lou ran a tight ship. The whole company, Peter, was like a family.''

"Any of these extra men—actors, stage manager, house crew, stagehands—pay you any special attention, make any kind of pass at you?"

"Peter, you know how the theater is. Everyone is 'darling,' and you kiss people hello and good-bye."

"The stagehands and the box-office people?"

"Good God, no." She frowned. "No, no one made a play for me, Peter. Everyone knew that Bob and I were—were close. I guess you'd say I had a no-trespassing sign on me. Bob was the star."

"And you were still legally married to Gavin. You might say you were 'surrounded.' "

"Yes."

"You've left out someone who must have had feelings about the company," Peter said. "The author. Was he happy with what Gavin and the actors did to his brainchild?"

"Reggie Stevens? Oh, he's a love, Peter. *Triangle* was his first shot at Broadway. He was a little in awe of everyone at first. But he was quick to accept suggestions for changes he liked, and stubborn about those he didn't. He was with us every hour of rehearsals, of course, and I guess he saw every performance for the first two weeks of the run. When he knew that *Triangle* might run forever he married his girlfriend and took off for Europe."

"He must wonder what hit him if he's heard the news," Peter said. "But he obviously wasn't breathing into your phone."

"Reggie? Of course he wasn't. I mean—"

"We're dealing with a sweetness-and-light world, a happy family, where everyone is suddenly under attack," Peter said. "Why, Deborah? You've got to get yourself pulled together, luv, because you have to know the answer. You're a target."

A man like Maxvil, whose life is devoted to a study of crime, collects what amounts to something like a series of clichés about criminal patterns. He has seen them all before and his reactions to them are conditioned by long experience.

"Peter is right," Maxvil told Deborah. "Somewhere, hidden away in your mind, there can be an answer to all this: why Robert Dale and Gavin Hayes have been murdered; why someone would try to keep you from remembering and telling us." He spoke quietly, without any effort to pressure the frightened woman. "It's possible that you know something that, at the moment, you don't remember that you know. Your visitor this morning thinks you do remember, or will remember."

"It's just not so," Deborah said. She sat very straight in a corner of the couch. Peter sat in the opposite corner. Maxvil faced her, perched on the corner of a stretcher table. He was smoking one of his inevitable cigarettes, his eyes narrowed as usual against the smoke. Patrolman Murphy had left to join his partner in a neighborhood search for a lingering pervert.

"We don't yet have a clue as to why Robert Dale was beaten to death," Maxvil said. "We don't have a clue as to why Gavin Hayes was shot. The two events could be unrelated. But now comes this attempt to get at you, the third person in a very closely knit group. Experience and instinct tell me that they have to relate. It's too great a coincidence to read any other way. You don't say 'It could be so-and-so. He hates me because—' You suggested Smallwood—who couldn't have been your caller, by the way. It couldn't have been Hayes, whom I suspected in the beginning in the Dale case. Hayes was dead when your phone call came and someone later knocked on your door. So we don't have any kind of lead—yet. But your caller thinks you know something that would point to him as a double murderer. What is it, Miss Wallace?"

She had done an admirable job of getting her hysteria under control, but she seemed almost frozen where she sat.

"I don't know!" It was an intense whisper. "For God's sake, Lieutenant, wouldn't I tell you if I did?"

"I think you would," Maxvil said. "I think you will when you remember. It's my job, Peter's job if he will, to take you back over your relationship with Dale and Hayes—probably over recent events, possibly way back—to help you find what we're looking for. You know, Miss Wallace, when I was a kid my mother was a chronic mislayer of things—like the key to the house, or her glasses, or a letter she'd gotten that day from a friend. 'I put it in a safe place,' she'd say. But she couldn't remember what the 'safe place' was. The mind is like that. It stores away unimportant—or so they seem at the time—facts, casual conversations, trivial incidents. They don't surface, may never surface again, unless something triggers your memory of them. We've got to find something to trigger that recall in you."

"I never mislay anything," Deborah said. Her husky voice had lost its color. "I am trained to remember words, conversations, actions, stage business. It's my profession. If Bob or Gavin had told me something that suggested they were in danger, I couldn't possibly forget it. I couldn't bury it away. They were the closest people to me in my life. I cared for them. I care, desperately, about what's happened to them." She was suddenly gripping the arm of the couch. "I couldn't forget anything that might be an answer. I *couldn't!*"

"I know you think that," Maxvil said. "Let's say for a moment that it's true, that you don't have anything stored away. Someone thinks you may have—your breather, your man at the door. He knows how close you were to Dale and Hayes. He thinks it's likely that one of them told you something that will point to him. He means to make sure that you don't tell us what he thinks you know. He knows you haven't told us yet or we'd have arrested him. He thinks you haven't put two and two together yet, but when you do you'll come up with his name. He's going to try to get to you before that happens.''

"What do I do?" Deborah cried out.

"Two things," Maxvil said. "You can't stay here alone. We've got to find some place to hide you away. And I still think there's a chance you may know something that hasn't rung a bell yet. I'd like to have Peter try to help you search for it, locate the safe place where you've hidden it.''

"Where can I hide?" Deborah asked.

"Give me a little time to work something out," Maxvil said. "Peter will stay here with you, and the cops will guard the building. Protective custody would be the most sensible thing, but I don't think you'd like it.''

"I'd die locked up in jail!''

"Maybe not, but it certainly wouldn't help you to remember something I hope is there to remember. You see, Miss Wallace, if you haven't got a clue hidden away in you, we're at square one, without a single damned signpost pointing anywhere.''

3

A man's home is his castle until it's invaded by the enemy, known or unknown. Peter thought he knew what Deborah Wallace was feeling. This apartment, where her private life was located, her pictures of friends, her clothes, her books and china and intimate knickknacks, had been a safe harbor. Now two of her friends stared down at her from the wall, both violently murdered. The doorbell, which had heralded the arrival of friends, now signaled danger, or, at least, strangers—the police, and next there might be reporters. She wanted to get away from here, and yet there was no safe place to go. The streets weren't safe. Until they had some clue to his identity the "breather" could be right behind her. Since he was likely to be someone she knew, no friend, no member of the disbanded *Triangle* company was above suspicion. The only person she had any reason to trust was Peter, an almost total stranger. He had to foster that trust in the hope that she would talk freely about the two men who had been so abruptly torn out of her life. Something one of them had said to her, casually, without special emphasis, might be the lead Maxvil needed so desperately.

They were alone in the no longer safe apartment. Maxvil had taken off to try to put the pieces of two murders together into recognizable shape. He would get back to them about a plan for Deborah's safety. Meanwhile Patrolmen Murphy and Kosufski were checking every visitor, every tradesman who had any reason to enter the brownstone on Thirty-eighth Street.

"It looks like you're stuck with me," Peter said.

Deborah had gone into the kitchen to make coffee. As she appeared in the door he could hear the pot starting to percolate behind her. She had done something to repair the ravages of tears, but fear was still reflected in her dark violet eyes. Peter's first reaction to her the day before had been that, without words, she was pleading for help. It was there now, and he had a strong impulse to provide it.

"I'm grateful it's you, Peter," she said. "Not some well-meaning friend who'd have no idea what to do. And what friend could I trust?"

"I'm afraid I have very little idea what to do, except to keep you from running risks—and try to find that 'safe place' in your mind where Maxvil thinks you've stored something away."

Her look had drifted past him to the wall of pictures, which was behind his chair. A little nerve twitched high up on her pale cheek. He realized that Bob Dale and Gavin Hayes were both looking at her from that wall.

"How can you—how can the lieutenant—imagine that I know something so crucial as the motive for this horror and—and could just forget it?"

"It could be there and not be recognized for what it is," Peter said. "A joke about someone; a piece of gossip about someone; an anecdote of some sort, told to you without Dale or Hayes guessing that it had any bearing on their futures."

98

"A joke!" she said. "An anecdote!' Her bitter little smile was a mirror of her pain. "And what about you, Peter?"

"What about me?"

"When you first came to see me—was it only yesterday?—you thought Bob might have been killed by mistake; that it had been meant for you."

He realized that since the moment when Maxvil had called him about Gavin Hayes, the thought that he might have been the original target had evaporated. He had accepted, without any really solid reasons, that the two murders were connected. That had taken him off the list of targets for this murderer in his own mind, and probably Maxvil's, since the detective hadn't mentioned it again or warned him to look out for his own safety.

"It doesn't seem likely anymore," he said.

"The man who's after me can know you're here, trying to get me to tell you something," Deborah said. "Doesn't that place you in danger?"

"Every policeman, every reporter who tries to track down a killer places himself in danger," Peter said. "It's the name of the game."

"But you can walk away from it," Deborah said. "Peter, I couldn't bear it if someone else I know and like was hurt because I won't or can't remember something. Let the police protect me—if they can. Don't run risks for me."

He smiled at her. "Would it surprise you to know that I find I care very much about what happens to you? So don't talk nonsense. We'll see this thing through to the end, wherever it takes us."

"Oh, Peter!" She came toward him, unsteadily, as though her center of balance weren't functioning. He stood up and took her in his arms to steady her. Hysteria was very near the surface again. "All the props have been ripped out from under my life," she said, clinging to him. "Gavin, who guided my career and made me a success; Bob, whom I loved. 'Never say forever,' Bob said. And the minute we did he was gone! Now there's only you, a stranger. It's not fair to you. I have no right to ask you—''

"You haven't asked me. I'm here by my own choice. When you were a kid didn't you ever have your fortune told with cards or tea leaves?''

"Tea leaves—?''

"Didn't the fortune teller tell you that a dark stranger was about to come into your life? So here I am." He brushed a strand of hair back from her forehead, smiling down at her. "That coffee must be just about done. And would you believe I haven't had anything to eat since yesterday's lunch? Is it possible there are a couple of eggs in your icebox and the makings of some toast?''

It worked. It was something for her to do. She tied an apron around her waist. Did he like his eggs dry or wet? She scrambled them to perfection, made toast and buttered it, and served the result in the little dining alcove off the kitchen. The coffee was equally perfect. He felt like a new man when he'd finished and pushed back his chair. She sat opposite him, lighting a cigarette for herself.

"I quit smoking every two weeks," he said. "Maybe I decided to cover this case because Maxvil is always well supplied. May I borrow one?''

"Don't I remember you carry a lighter?'' she asked.

"Just in case I change my mind suddenly I want to be prepared," he said. The damned cigarette tasted marvelous after food and coffee. He spoke very casually. "Let me give you an idea of the kind of thing Maxvil is looking for from you, luv. Suppose Gavin or Bob said to you, 'Old Bert Brown in the box-office is probably stealing Jake Goldman blind.' ''

"That's absurd," Deborah said. "Bert Brown is solid as a rock.''

100

"So if it was said, you'd dismiss it, right? But suppose Brown is stealing from his employer, and suppose Bob and Gavin got the goods on him, threatened to expose him? Brown would have a motive then, wouldn't he? But you, who dismissed the original remark as absurd, have no reason to recall it now unless it appears in a new perspective."

"Do you really think—?"

"About Bert Brown? Of course I don't. I'm just trying to give you an example of the kind of thing that may have escaped you. So let's talk about your casual conversations with Bob and Gavin."

At Homicide in downtown Manhattan a young man named Wilfred Joyce sat in a cubbyhole of a little office playing with wooden blocks. He was called the Professor by his co-workers. Owlish horn-rimmed glasses and a lean, stooped figure seemed to justify the tag. The little wooden blocks on the table had letters pasted on them—D, H, and W. The Professor moved them around like an anagram player, trying to make words out of them. In addition to the wooden blocks there were a sheaf of reports on the table and a yellow legal pad on which the Professor made notes. Technically, the Professor's job was to analyze reports made by Lieutenant Maxvil, Sergeant Burke, and others from the fingerprint and photography crews and the medical examiner's office.

"Everything tells me, Willy," Maxvil had said to him, "that the murders of Dale and Hayes are part of one pattern. See what you can do to prove me right or wrong. We'll feed you more material as we collect it."

And so the Professor read the reports, and made notes, and then began fiddling with his wooden blocks; D for Dale, H for Hayes, and W for Wallace. He moved his blocks under the heading CAREERS. They all belonged there. Gavin Hayes had started a little earlier than the others, the boy wonder on Broadway. Dale had joined Hayes in a road company of one of Hayes's plays. From then on they had been close, first in films and finally in *Triangle* on Broadway.

Deborah Wallace had joined both men in the film from which Fay Douglas had removed herself. From then on her career had been moulded and guided by Gavin Hayes, and she was finally working again with both men in *Triangle*. From a career point of view the three people had been periodically together over a fifteen-year span.

Under the heading PERSONAL LIVES the three blocks came together again. Deborah Wallace and Robert Dale had been lovers at both ends of that time span, and W and H had been married in between. During the periods when Deborah Wallace and Dale had conducted a love affair, both of their relationships with Hayes had remained undisturbed. Hayes had known that the love affair would start again when they joined forces for *Triangle*. Even though he was still legally married to Deborah that hadn't bothered him.

The Professor made a note: "Hayes's marriage seems to have been an attempt to try a more conventional life-style. It didn't work. But his ambivalence doesn't seem to have disrupted his friendship with either Dale or Deborah, or his professional relationship with them. Thirty years ago, in the McCarthy period, an off-beat personality might have been considered a security risk. State Department people would sell out to the enemy, it was believed, rather than have their private lives revealed."

Under a heading THE CRIMES the Professor scribbled more notes. "Both men murdered in the early hours of the morning, between 2 and 5 A.M.—Neither victim apparently offered any resistance. Dale would certainly have been capable, but you suggest he was asleep and never had an inkling of what was about to happen to him. I buy that—"

*

"Access to Peter Styles's apartment and to backstage at the Boswell Theater suggests a prior knowledge of the territory. A friend of Styles's who also knew the backstage area at the Boswell? What about the woman, Deborah Wallace? She was working at the Boswell and carrying on an affair with Dale in Styles's apartment. You only have her word for it that there was a 'breather' and a man at the door of her apartment. That's not quite accurate, is it? The lady on the third floor says a man spoke to her when she called down to find out who she'd let in. Who, beside the Wallace girl in the *Triangle* company was familiar with Styles's place? Worth asking.

"Hayes was working at his desk when he was shot. Either he didn't see who shot him, or if he did, he had no notion that his caller was dangerous. He made no move to protect himself—"

Maxvil was not a man who waited for bright young analysts in the department to tell him which end was up in a case. While the Professor wrote his notes about finding out who in the *Triangle* company was familiar with Peter Styles's apartment, Maxvil was already asking the question.

Everyone connected with *Triangle* had been summoned to the Boswell Theater: actors, stage manager, stagehands, box-office treasurer and his staff, Jake Goldman, the owner of the building, and McNamara, the night watchman. The only persons involved and not present were Reginald Stevens, the author, who was honeymooning in Europe, and Deborah Wallace.

The houselights were on in the theater's auditorium, the glaring work light over the stage. All the people summoned sat down in the first few rows, with the exception of Lou Nason, the stage manager. Nason had set up a card table on stage and he and Maxvil sat at it. The stage manager, a dark, bright-eyed little man, had made a list of all the people

103

and was identifying them to Maxvil. There were two women, the pretty blond ingenue, Sandra Lake, and a plain-looking girl, wearing steel-rimmed granny-glasses, named Betty Jessup, who worked in the box office. The two other actors, Eddie Marks, the juvenile, and Joe Becket, who had replaced Lucien Smallwood during rehearsals, were unremarkable except for Becket's size. Physically, he was almost as big as Smallwood, but younger and less dissipated. The stagehands, five of them, were just faces. Bert Brown, the box-office treasurer, was a tall, dignified-looking man, who was obviously wearing a sandy-colored toupee. In his sixties, Maxvil thought.

Jake Goldman, who owned this theater and a dozen others, was short, squat, with dark hair turned gray at the sides. A cigar, which he rolled between false teeth from one corner of his mouth to the other, was something to chew on, not to smoke. If you asked him, he'd tell you he'd given up smoking some years back but found the cigar was a part of his image he couldn't do without. His father and his brothers before him had been cigar smokers. A Goldman without that aggressive cigar would have somehow lost authority. He sat apart from everyone else, one leg crossed over the other, jerking back and forth impatiently. No one gave Jake Goldman orders, and he tried to make that clear to Maxvil.

"We can't stay here all day, Lieutenant," he called out from his aisle seat in the house.

"I don't think it will take all day, Mr. Goldman," Maxvil said. "But if it does . . ." He smiled, and watched the cigar move to the other corner of Goldman's mouth.

Nason, the stage manager, pushed his list in front of Maxvil. "That's it, Lieutenant. Only Debbie Wallace and Reggie Stevens are absent."

Maxvil looked out at the faces below him. Tension

everywhere, he thought. He gave them something to be tense about.

"Miss Wallace, you've noticed, isn't here," he said. "That's because someone attempted to break into her apartment this morning. We have her under police protection."

"Oh, my God!" It was the blond girl. She reached out to grab the arm of Eddie Marks, the juvenile, who sat next to her.

"We have to believe that the two murders and the attempt on Miss Wallace are all part of one pattern," Maxvil said. "All three victims are connected with this play, this production. We have to believe that whoever found his way to Gavin Hayes's office on the fifth floor here was familiar with the theater, this building, the routines of the night watchman. Bob Dale, I'm sure you all know, was living in an apartment on Irving Place that belongs to Peter Styles, a reporter. The person who killed Dale had to know that Styles's place was a garden apartment, that there was a way in over a back fence into that garden and into the apartment without forcing any doors, risking being seen by any other tenants. If we are right in assuming that we are dealing with one killer, then it has to be someone who knew both places. How many of you here know Peter Styles or have ever been to his apartment?"

Dead silence. People looked at each other, waiting for an answer that didn't come.

"Dale, I understand, was very pleased to get an apartment," Maxvil said. "He didn't like living in a hotel. Did he ever describe Styles's place to any of you?"

Maxvil found himself watching Sandra Lake. It was just possible that Dale might have taken her to Peter's place, if Dale were playing two sides of the street at once. And it was the girl who spoke.

"He invited all of us for drinks and food the first Saturday night he had the apartment. Just the acting company and Lou Nason," she said.

Maxvil consulted the list Nason had made him. "That would be you, Miss Lake, and Mr. Marks, Mr. Becket, and Miss Wallace, along with Mr. Nason?"

"I forgot," she said. "Gavin was there, too."

"So you all knew about the garden, the French doors, in effect, a back way in?"

"Why the hell would anybody want to know about a back way in?" Joe Becket demanded. He had a big voice, like Smallwood's.

"To get to Dale to kill him," Maxvil said quietly.

"You like to scare the shit out of people, Mr. Lieutenant?" Jake Goldman asked. "You got some sensible questions to ask, ask them, and let's get out of here."

"I'm not accusing any of you," Maxvil said, "or trying to scare you. But the fact remains that six of you—five with Gavin Hayes gone—knew the layout there. I assume it was a lively party, you had a good time?"

"Bob was a marvelous host," Eddie Marks, the juvenile, said.

"So it isn't unnatural that you may have talked about the party to other people, and about the apartment Dale was so pleased to have. People in this theater now, friends outside of this group. If you did talk to anyone about it, do you recall anyone who had any special interest in the layout of the Styles apartment?"

There was silence for a moment, and then Sandra Lake spoke again.

"I may have talked about it to people," she said. "You can't know what it is like—was like—playing in a show with a big star like Bob Dale. Everybody was curious about him, wanted to know everything you could tell them about him."

"He was about the only big star I've ever known that

nobody had a bad word for," Joe Becket said.

"Except that he screwed every woman that ever came within three feet of him," Jake Goldman said, rolling his cigar from east to west.

"I'm afraid I must claim to be an exception," Sandra Lake said, color rising in her cheeks.

"Well, good for you, baby," Goldman said. "But your time would have come, you can be sure of that."

Maxvil ignored that exchange. "None of you remember any undue curiosity about the layout of Styles's apartment?"

No one did.

"Obviously all of you were familiar with the theater here."

"And let me give you an idea, Mr. Lieutenant," Jake Goldman said, "of how many other people are familiar with it. This theater was built in 1908! Since it first opened with an English play starring Forbes-Robertson there have been over three hundred productions in this house, involving thousands of actors, stagehands, directors, stage managers, business staffs, costumers, set designers, stage carpenters, ushers, and God knows who else, many of them still alive! Thousands more have come backstage to visit. A successful theater is as familiar to swarms of people as Grand Central Station is to commuters. And I suggest to you that those brownstones on Irving Place where Styles's apartment is were built around the turn of the century and are familiar to hundreds and hundreds of living people who aren't in this company and didn't have to find about them last week at a party—or last month! You could grow old following that line, Mr. Lieutenant."

"Were there quarrels within the company?" Maxvil asked, without commenting on Jake Goldman's outburst.

"The first day of rehearsal," Nason, the stage manager,

said, "Bob Dale complained about an actor named Smallwood, who turned up drunk. Mr. Hayes fired him. Joe Becket was hired to take his place. After that I've never worked in a company that had fewer problems."

"Why not?" Jake Goldman said. He seemed bent on obstruction. "Dale had a warmed-over girlfriend. He didn't have to steal from anyone else. That's usually where the troubles start, big star choosing whatever woman he wants. In this case it was the co-producer's wife."

"A nice motive," Maxvil said, "except that both men are dead. There are other motives for violence besides women, Mr. Goldman. The most prominent, I suggest, is money. Gavin Hayes leased this theater from you. What were your dealings with him?"

"Routine," Goldman said. "You understand about theaters, Mr. Lieutenant? You lease to a producer for the run of his play. You have the play read, you find out about the star and the cast. If you think the play will run, you take the gamble, because you can't collect rent after it closes— like now! You guess wrong and you have a dark house on your hands. It's not like the twenties when there were dozens of producers clamoring for a theater. This house can be dark for the rest of the season."

"But you got along all right with Hayes?"

"It was the two of them, Hayes and Dale," Goldman said. "They put up their own money, which is unusual. Producers usually have dozens of investors, keeping their own money safe. Bob Dale was so popular that this play seemed surefire. And it is—was—goddamn it! Now we have refunds to make and I suppose Hayes's and Dale's money will be tied up in probate for God knows how long. You can bet your sweet life, Mr. Lieutenant, that whatever I may have thought of Bob Dale and Gavin Hayes personally, I wanted them alive. This play was a potential gold mine. It would have paid the rent on this house for a long time, and collecting rents is my business."

"We've only had two problems with *Triangle*." It was Bert Brown, the box-office treasurer with the toupee, who spoke. "We couldn't meet the demand for tickets after we opened, and now we've got trouble making refunds. Everyone connected with it is suddenly out of work—when they expected to be safe for a year or two. Everything depended on Bob Dale staying alive and healthy." He permitted himself a nervous little laugh. "If anyone here wanted Bob Dale dead, he'd have waited till after the run was over."

Maxvil lit a cigarette and sat looking down at the cast, the crew, the house management, and the owner. He thought of show business, the theater, as a world of gossip. Gossip about people from Hollywood to Broadway kept syndicated columnists, whole magazines, TV and radio talk-show hosts and hostesses alive. Gossip was big business in itself. But in the last thirty-six hours he had heard only one juicy bit beyond the general talk about Bob Dale's womanizing. That had come from Sam Cowley, Peter's aged friend at The Players. Old Sam had suggested that Dale may have had something on Gavin Hayes, long ago, and used it to promote his own career. Once a blackmailer, always a blackmailer, Maxvil thought. But "long ago" didn't make much sense. Dale's career had been an enormous success. If he had turned the screws on Gavin Hayes way back when, it was no longer necessary. Dale had become a very rich man, could pick his own spots without turning on any heat. His success had contributed to Hayes's success. They had been partners in this final venture. Their individual relationships with Deborah Wallace had apparently caused no frictions. The one person, so far, who had had it in for both Dale and Hayes was Lucien Smallwood, the drunken actor.

109

Sergeant Burke was at work trying to pick up Smallwood's trail for the last two days, and Maxvil was ready to bet that Smallwood would prove to be in the clear. So far there was nothing that pointed anywhere else.

Maxvil stood up and spoke to the assembled company. "I need your help," he said. "Somewhere in Robert Dale's past or even his recent present is a person who hated him beyond anything we can think of as normal. He wasn't just eliminated. The person who killed him crept into his bedroom while he was asleep and beat him to death—beat him and beat him long after the job was done. The fury of that attack tells me that we are dealing with a dangerous psychotic. Someone that far around-the-bend will go to any lengths to protect himself. I have to think that Gavin Hayes had some clue to the identity of the killer which he kept to himself. It cost him his life. The killer believes that Deborah Wallace, close to both men, may have the same clue. He has made a clumsy attempt to get at her. We are trying to help her to remember what it is she may know. But I want to say to all of you what we have said to Miss Wallace. Any of you may have heard something, seen something, been told something about some quarrel, some grudge, which could point to the killer. I urge you to tell us anything that comes to mind, no matter how outlandish it may seem to you, because to keep quiet about it may result in your finding yourselves on this madman's list of victims." He put out his cigarette in a saucer that Nason had provided as an ashtray. "Talk to each other, try to remember anything you may have heard about Bob Dale's life that could have resulted in such hatred. People have talked about men whose women he stole. Who were they? Where are they? Don't make judgments about what makes sense and what doesn't make sense. Because nothing about this makes sense in a normal way. If you talk, speculate in public about

110

this, you may be placing yourselves in a very real danger. Bring it to me, instead. In the back of the auditorium is Sergeant Parker." Heads turned. "He will be stationed here until our work at the theater is done. Tell him anything that comes to mind. It's for your own sakes, not just to help the police. Thank you for your attention."

"Tell me, Mr. Lieutenant," Jake Goldman called out, "how long do you propose to occupy this theater?"

"Till we have covered every inch of it, till we have looked in every cupboard, in every drawer, in every desk, in every trashcan, in the box-office safe, in the scene dock, the tool chests, the costume rooms, the private toilets, the public rest rooms, the elevator shaft, perhaps even under the floor boards."

"What are you looking for, Mr. Lieutenant?"

"I wish to God I could tell you, Mr. Goldman," Maxvil said. "A gun, perhaps; a piece of cloth torn from a suit; a cigar ash that doesn't belong where it is; a strand of hair; a broken lock; a forced window or door."

"Maybe the killer left you a calling card," Jake Goldman said, cigar rolling. He expected laughter but he didn't get it.

"Maybe he did, Mr. Goldman," Maxvil said.

A safe place to hide Deborah Wallace was suggested by an unexpected source. A hotel or busy apartment building would not do; people coming and going with no way to check on them. In the early afternoon Peter, still with Deborah in her apartment, called Frank Devery at *Newsview* to bring him up to date. It was his boss who reminded Peter that on the roof of the Newsview Building on Madison Avenue there was a penthouse apartment. Devery used it himself when some all-night news story was about to break. Elevators in the building only went to the floor below. You reached the roof by a narrow fire stair. There was no traffic to the roof. One man could guard that stairway. The building itself was closed to the general public after seven in the evening. No one could go up from the lobby level without passing the night guards, giving his name, and stating his business. No one but Devery and the building superintendent had a key to the penthouse; no one had reason or any business to go there.

"We can slip her up there without anyone seeing her and that will be that," Devery said. "No way some crazy man can get to her. If Maxvil handles it right, there's no way he could guess where you've taken her. We can turn the whole bloody building into a fortress if necessary."

It appeared ideal to Peter, and when he was able to reach Maxvil the detective agreed. They would wait until the Newsview Building was closed to the public at seven. They would whisk Deborah away from her place in a police car. If "the breather" was still in the neighborhood, he'd have no way to follow. There'd be a second patrol car waiting for just that to happen. The killer would have to assume, if he were there, that Deborah was being placed in protective custody.

Maxvil, along with Sergeant Burke, arrived at Deborah's apartment just before seven. She was packing a bag, going into hiding behind those black glasses once again.

"So you've spent all day with her," Maxvil said.

"Nothing. Her life story, much about both Dale and Hayes, but nothing useful," Peter said.

"Maybe she doesn't really know anything."

"That doesn't make her safe if the killer thinks otherwise," Peter said. "What about you?"

"Nothing so far," Maxvil said. "Some 'could be's.' Hayes was shot with a .44-caliber handgun. We have the bullet, but no ballistics record of it in the police department

112

here or at the FBI in Washington. The medical examiner thinks Dale may have been beaten to death with a gun butt. There were some traces of oil in the garbage of his brain. Could be the same weapon was used in both cases, but no way to prove it. Nothing at the Boswell Theater. No sign of a break-in. The killer knew his way in and out. He either had a way to get in at the time—two A.M.—or he got into the theater much earlier, when there was traffic, and waited for his moment. Could be either one.''

"The men who've been watching this building?''

"Nothing. No one suspicious hanging around the neighborhood.''

"The other people in the *Triangle* company?''

"I tried to scare them into talking," Maxvil said, "but either I didn't do a good job or they drew the same blank Miss Wallace is drawing.''

Deborah, hidden behind her glasses, came out of the bedroom, carrying a small bag. However much Peter had managed to relax her during the day, it was gone now. Her lips trembled as she spoke.

"Do I have to stay alone in an empty building?'' she asked. "My God, Lieutenant, I'm so damned scared!''

"Not alone, luv," Peter said. He smiled at her. "We've only just begun to talk.''

"Oh, Peter, Peter! There's nothing, I tell you. Nothing to remember.''

"It'll pop in time," Peter said. "You'll see.''

A black limousine waited outside the brownstone. A patrol car was pulled in behind it. Deborah, walking between Peter and Maxvil, was hustled across the sidewalk and into the rear seat of the limousine. The car took off.

"I've always loved this neighborhood," Deborah said. "It seemed friendly, safe. Now—''

"No one is going to follow you, Miss Wallace," Maxvil

said. "I wish he'd try and we'd nail him."

Maxvil had made arrangements with Devery. Deborah was to be taken to the side entrance of the Newsview Building, away from the Madison Avenue traffic. At this hour the delivery trucks that used that side entrance were through for the day. Devery himself waited for them. Deborah crossed the sidewalk from the limousine and slipped into the building. She acknowledged an introduction to *Newsview*'s publisher and stepped into a freight elevator. In addition to Peter and Maxvil, they were joined by a plainclothes cop.

"This is Sergeant Croft," Maxvil said to Deborah. "He will be the first of three men who'll guard the stairway to the roof. He'll be relieved at midnight by another officer who'll be introduced to you by Croft, so you'll have no uncertainty about who's guarding you. There'll be another change of guards at eight in the morning. The new man will be identified to you. The only person with free access to you, without special permission from me, will be Peter. If there is any reason for someone else to see you personally, I'll be on the telephone to alert you."

"Is it—am I really in so much danger?" Deborah asked.

"We will assume it till we know you're not," Maxvil said.

The elevator moved noiselessly to the top of the shaft. The four men and Deborah stepped out into the hallway of the thirty-sixth floor. It was deserted, quiet. Devery led the way to an iron fire door over which a little red electric sign burned.

"The only way to the roof, Miss Wallace," Devery said, opening the door. "There's no access to the roof from adjoining buildings. We are higher than any other building around us."

They climbed the narrow stairway. At the top was

another door, which led out onto the roof. The penthouse, like a small cottage, stood in the center of it. Devery used his key to let them in.

The interior consisted of a pleasant, fairly large living room, two bedrooms separated by a bath, and a kitchenette. Devery, who was a sports freak, had decorated the living-room walls with old Currier and Ives sporting prints. The room was uncluttered. A typewriter and a flat-topped desk were the only suggestions that the apartment had a special purpose.

"In the kitchenette there is a coffeepot and coffee," Devery said. "There are a few frozen dinners in the icebox. There's an ice maker and enough booze in the pantry to last you a month. If you have to stay here longer than tonight, you can give Peter a list of things you find you need."

"Sergeant Croft will be set up outside the fire door on the thirty-sixth floor," Maxvil said. "You can lock and chain-bolt the door to this apartment from the inside. When you are alone be sure that you do just that.

"There are two telephones there on the desk," Devery said. "The black one is an outside line. The red one connects with the magazine switchboard. That switchboard is manned twenty-four hours a day in case you want to contact anyone in the building."

"Who would I want to contact in the building?" Deborah asked.

"Me," Devery said. "Peter, if he should leave you to work in his office."

"Only Peter, Mr. Devery, and the police know that you're here, Miss Wallace," Maxvil said. "I'd prefer you didn't use that red phone unless there's an emergency we don't expect."

"The security people who cover the building at night are going to know something is up when they see me in the hall downstairs," Sergeant Croft said.

"So let 'em guess what it is," Maxvil said. "You can tell them the police are guarding the penthouse without saying why, can't you, Devery?"

"Yes."

"I don't believe you could be safer anywhere except in jail," Maxvil said. "Keep talking to Peter, won't you, Miss Wallace? I still think something will come to the surface that could help us."

Peter and Deborah were left alone in the penthouse. Peter locked the door and put the chain bolt in place.

"Make you a drink? I know I need one," Peter said.

"If there is vodka—and tonic," Deborah said.

Hours of talk had left Peter discouraged. He was certain Deborah was not consciously resisting, but nothing in all the stories she'd told him about herself, about Dale and Hayes and their lives together, had produced anything that threw a glimmer of light on the murders. Or if something had surfaced he had missed it.

Devery's liquor supply was as promised. Peter made a vodka and tonic for Deborah and a bourbon on the rocks for himself and carried the drinks back into the living room. Deborah was curled up in the corner of the couch, looking more like a bedraggled little girl than a glamorous actress. She had taken off her black glasses and put them on the coffee table in front of the couch.

"I'm exhausted from all this talk about me, and Bob, and Gavin," she said. "Do you still think I've buried something inside me, Peter?"

"It's possible. Why else your 'breather'?"

"It could be something he thinks I know that *I don't* know!"

"Also possible."

"Oh, Peter, let's take a rest. Let's talk about something

116

else—politics, the wars all over the world. Let's talk about you."

"A long and rather bitter business," he said, his face muscles tightening.

"I know about your wife," she said. "How awful for you."

"And for her."

It never came up without his feeling that someone had just run a knife into his guts.

"But—but there's more," she said. "Bob told me—about your leg. I—I've watched you, and it's hard to believe. I mean, you don't have the slightest limp. If it hadn't all been made so public, no one would ever guess."

"Modern engineering," he said, his voice gone hard.

"There were some old copies of *Newsview* in your apartment," she said. "Fifteen years old. I remembered when I saw them that this awful thing had happened to you around the same time that Bob and I came together, so full of joy and life. Perhaps I read about it at the time, but I was so involved with a love affair that what happened to anyone else was of no consequence at all." She reached out to him. "Don't talk about it if it's too painful."

"You asked," he said, his voice harsh.

He reached down and pulled up his right trouser leg, revealing an artificial leg and foot, attached just below his knee by a leather harness. He gave it an impatient slap and then lowered his trouser leg. He heard her breath draw in with a little gasp.

"Satisfied?" he asked, and carried his drink across the room to the window, looking out over the roofs of the city, bathed in a late-summer twilight. Damn people's curiosity. He realized he was breathing hard, as though he'd been running.

117

"I wish I could cut out my tongue," Deborah said in a small voice.

He turned. She looked, he thought, as if he had struck her. Why had he made such a production of it? It had to do, he guessed, with her mention of Grace his wife. It was Grace who, years ago, stripped him of his self-pity. It was Grace who had lifted a burden from him, taught him to make love again without shyness, without feeling that he was some kind of curiosity. For God's sake, there were thousands of war veterans, amputees, who lived normal lives without feeling they were freaks. He could have shown Deborah his leg, laughed about it, lifted her embarrassment. Instead he had made her natural curiosity into some kind of villainy.

He walked over and sat down beside her on the couch.

"I'm sorry," he said. "Drink your drink. There are moments when violence turns me on. It's been all around me for the last two days—what happened to Dale, to Hayes, and what may have been meant to happen to you. It brings back what happened to me, and to Grace, and it makes me sick and angry."

"I don't know how I could have been so stupid," she said. "But I was so weary of talking about myself, and Bob, and Gavin. I was trying to find some way to get us on to some other subject for awhile. Please forgive me, Peter. Please!"

He reached out and covered her hand with his. "There's nothing to forgive," he said. "You're right, of course. Persisting in digging for something buried away may actually shut the door on it. Talking about something else may uncover it when we least expect it." He took a sip of his drink and felt his own tensions retreating. After all it had been what seemed like a lifetime ago—a marriage ago.

"I was a bright young man-about-town," he told Deb-

118

orah, "writing witty pieces about New York's night life and all the beautiful people who hang out in all the classy saloons in town." He glanced at her. "I was going to be the greatest young American novelist since Hemingway, but the saloon pieces for *Newsview* kept me eating. Winter weekends I often went skiing up in Vermont." His mouth tightened. "One week I didn't come back in one piece. Some crazy kids tried to play passing games with me coming down a mountain on the way home. Maybe I didn't have the nerve for the kind of games crazy kids played in the sixties. My car smashed through the guard rail and somersaulted down a steep hill, burning. I—I was thrown clear."

He paused, reliving it in spite of himself. "I came to in a hospital in Bennington, and my leg was gone. I remember shouting for the doctor, threatening to kill him. He should have given me some choice. I know now that he had no choice. My leg had been shattered beyond repair." Peter drew a deep breath. "It was the end of the world, my world. I felt loathsome, repulsive. Of course, it was months and months before they could think of building an artificial leg for me. I walked with crutches, not wanting to leave my apartment. My good friend, Frank Devery, stayed with me in some of my suicidal moments, always trying to get me back to work. I couldn't write the kind of smart-aleck column I'd been doing before it happened. There was no wit or humor left in me. I had only one wish in the whole world, to find those two boys in the sports car and kill them for what they had done to me."

"You never found them?"

Peter shook his head, slowly. "But in the process of looking for them I became aware of how much senseless violence there is in today's world—man's inhumanity to man. I became an investigative reporter on the subject for *News-*

view. Then there was Grace, who became a sort of partner, and then a lover, and then a wife. And then—she, too—mowed down by some fanatical kids in a camp for Vietnamese refugees she was trying to help. So you see, Deborah, for me the music has gone round and round and seems always to come out at the same place. That's why I'm here, because I don't want it to happen to you—or to anyone else on this earth.''

He got up to refill their drinks. He felt better for having told it. She watched him as he brought back the glasses, unable not to notice that there was no limp, no trace of awkwardness.

He grinned at her. ''Magical springs and hinges, better than the original,'' he said.

It was as if they had shared an emotional experience. It was as if they were suddenly old friends. Talk was easy, not a straining effort to remember something. Deborah did the bulk of that talking, about her childhood, her parents, the beginnings of her career as an apprentice in summer stock, an early romance. But always Peter managed to steer her back to that part of her life that involved Bob Dale and Gavin Hayes.

''Bob was something new that is taking place in films and theater,'' she said at one point. ''Earlier generations had romantic leading men like John Gilbert, John Barrymore, Leslie Howard, Charles Boyer, and others of that stripe—handsome, elegant, with a dramatic flare that drove the ladies up the wall. Spencer Tracy was, I suppose, one of the first male stars who wasn't what you'd call 'beautiful' who had a tremendous appeal.''

''Clark Gable?''

''Handsome, brash, very male, but not with the style of a Barrymore or a Howard,'' Deborah said. ''I wasn't old enough to be had by that earlier generation. Tracy and

120

Gable and Gary Cooper were my teenage idols. Bob was like Tracy; no Greek god, but with a personality that lit up the whole landscape. He'll still be breaking hearts as long as they show his movies on the late-late TV shows.''

"There must be enormous jealousy of a man who has so much appeal."

Deborah hesitated. "Not from people who worked with him, I think. He was so damned professional. I think actors admire that more than anything else in other actors. He never had trouble with lines, never had to be told twice how to implement a director's suggestion. But most of all he was professional about his work routines. I don't suppose he was ever late in his life for a call, and on film location you can be called as early as five thirty in the morning for makeup. If anyone was late and managed to hold up everyone else, Bob would call him, or her, down in a way they were never likely to forget. When he had made it as a star he was always the first person on the set, whether it was required of him or not. He wouldn't ask anyone to do anything he wasn't prepared to do himself. That didn't go just for actors. He demanded total professionalism from cameramen, grips, makeup people—down to the script girl and the boy who went for coffee, the gofer. But he was just as quick to heap praise on people who did the smallest job well. He would defend fellow actors from a bullying director. No one who ever worked in a film with Bob—or a play for that matter—could ever say, seriously, that he was unfairly treated by him, or ever failed to get praise and applause when he deserved it. A very special man to work with."

Every time they talked about Dale he came up smelling like a rose, Peter thought. A strong man, a fair man, so fair that it was hard to imagine someone hating him enough to bludgeon him to death. Even a man like Smallwood would have to admit that Dale's treatment of him was justified. But a psychotic wouldn't care about justification. Or was it possible that Deborah, so deeply involved with Dale, was blind to any negative aspects of his character?

The talk about Gavin Hayes had mostly to do with the sides of him that Deborah had found amusing—his passion for fancy clothes, his jewelry, which he wore in profusion when he was in his own surroundings, his witty bitchiness about almost everyone, his great skills as a director in getting the best out of people who worked under him. Quite different from Dale, he could fly into a temper, tell people off who didn't deserve it, fight with producers or studio executives for no sensible reason, accuse people of things they hadn't done, be totally obnoxious. But when the film was in the can or the play opened, the people who had worked for him knew he had gotten the best from them they had to give. That went for writers and technicians, who battled with him before the fact, as well as actors. In the end not only was Gavin Hayes's reputation enhanced, but so were the reputations of all the other people involved.

"People felt, I think, that it was worth enduring his tantrums, his snide comments, his gossipy needle, to achieve what he got out of them," Deborah said. She shook her head. "Ever since yesterday I've been telling myself I could have understood the terrible violence of Bob's death if it had been directed at Gavin. He was a genius at making enemies while, at the same time, he produced successes for the enemies he made."

"I'm convinced he was a secondary target for the killer," Peter said. "I think he guessed who hated Dale so much and kept it a secret too long. The killer thinks you know the same secret, I'm afraid."

They had more drinks, and coffee, and some frozen fish sticks browned in the oven. Suddenly there was a sharp

122

knock at the door. Peter glanced at his watch. It was midnight. They'd been talking and talking.

It was Sergeant Croft at the door. Peter undid the chain bolt and the door lock. There was a short, sandy-haired man with Croft who was introduced as Officer Loomis.

"Loomis is taking over for me from now till eight in the morning," Croft said. "Lieutenant Maxvil wanted you to meet him so you'd know who was guarding you—in case."

Loomis looked coldly efficient. He made no bones about the gun he was carrying in a shoulder holster under his suitcoat.

"You planning to leave in a while, Mr. Styles?" he asked. "I don't want to be surprised by someone moving around."

He and Deborah had run out of energy for any more talk, any more probing for some hidden information, Peter thought.

"Yes, I'll be going in a few minutes," he said.

"Peter, must you?" Deborah asked in a very small voice. "I don't want to be left alone. Could you stay? There's a second bedroom. It will be different when it's daylight."

He looked at her. There was nothing coy, nothing devious about her. She was just plain scared.

"Sure, I'll stay," he said.

The two policemen left, Loomis to take up the post at the foot of the fire stairs. Peter and Deborah had a nightcap. She wasn't the kind of woman, he thought, you'd normally spend the night with and not make some sort of a pass. She was too attractive for the thought not to occur. But tonight she was a child, exhausted by tragedy. Sex wasn't why she'd asked him to stay. There was no danger with Loomis standing guard, but there was the fear of being isolated from anyone she knew, anyone she could call "friend." Peter thought he understood that. His presence was little enough to give in the situation.

"In the theater everyone is 'darling'—you kiss hello and good-bye," she had said.

They checked the two bedrooms and she chose the one she wanted. Its windows looked out toward the blinking lights on the East River. The bathroom, which they would have to share, was equipped with a new toothbrush, a razor, and shaving cream. Devery sometimes used the apartment to house a writer doing a special feature for them. It was equipped for emergencies.

"So sleep well," Peter said. "Try to forget the whole thing until we start over again—tomorrow."

He kissed her good-night on the forehead and went to his own room. He realized he was dead tired. It had been a long forty-eight hours. He took off his coat, switched off the bedside lamp, and lay down on the top of the bed.

He was out, almost before his head touched the pillow.

And then, much later, she was screaming.

He was down so deep in the well of sleep that he acted purely from instinct. He sprang out of bed—and fell flat on his face. In some kind of fog after he had first gone out, he must have raised up later and taken off his artificial leg. It had been paining him during the evening, and taking it off was almost automatic.

She was still screaming.

He fumbled for the light, couldn't find it, couldn't find where he had put the leg, and hopped into the bathroom and into Deborah's room. There was a violent struggle taking place on her bed. City lights provided little visibility, but enough for him to see a dark shadow pounding at Deborah.

He hopped forward, shouting at the top of his lungs. The shadow turned and lunged at Peter. Unable to balance himself, Peter went down under a powerful blow to the side of his head. The shadow disappeared—out the bedroom window and onto the roof.

Deborah was surely a woman of courage. She found the light and, her face bleeding and bruised, ran to Peter. He was already struggling up.

"He was suddenly there!" she said.

"Are you all right?"

"Oh my God, Peter, I'm not sure. But you—?"

"I'm a damn fool," he said.

She steadied him back to his room, where he found the artificial leg, which had fallen under the bed. He strapped it on, not concerned that she stood in the doorway, watching.

The attacker must still be out on the roof, though how he had gotten there was a question. The chain and the lock on the door were undisturbed. The man had come through Deborah's window.

"It never occurred to me," she said. "It was warm. I—I wanted fresh air."

"He had to get by Loomis," Peter said.

He took a poker from the fire irons in the living room. Over protests from Deborah he went out onto the roof. He wanted to find the bastard. No sign of anyone. He went to the fire stairs and called down to Loomis.

No answer.

He went down the stairs and opened the lower door.

The policeman lay in a pool of blood in the inside hallway.

PART THREE

1

There was an ugly wound at the back of Officer Loomis's head, but he was breathing, alive. Peter went along the dimly lit hallway trying a succession of office doors. He wanted to get to a switchboard phone to get help from the building's night crew. The man who had slugged Loomis and made his way into Deborah's room could still be somewhere in the building. God knows how badly Loomis was hurt. He was certainly in need of medical help. Every door Peter tried was locked. Neat people, *Newsview*'s employees.

He ran back up the fire stairs to the roof and pounded on the penthouse door.

"It's Peter!"

Deborah let him in. She was holding a wet cloth to her bruised face.

He went to the red phone, got the switchboard, alerted night security. Then on the black phone he dialed Maxvil's home number, one he knew well. The detective sounded sleepy and angry when he answered. He had needed sleep as much as anyone else.

"Jesus!" was all he said when Peter told him what had happened. The line went dead. He was on his way.

Peter turned away from the phones and put his arms around Deborah. Her whole body was shaking.

"I wasn't doing very well with sleeping," she said, fighting tears. "On and off—every little sound seemed to wake me. But I must have dozed off and then—I woke and he was coming through the window."

"You get a look at him—at his face?"

"No. What little light there was was behind him. I—I sat up, the sheet and blanket pulled around me, and screamed. He rushed at me. He had a gun in his right hand. He didn't shoot because I guess he couldn't see me very clearly. He raised the weapon to strike at me, and somehow I managed to get that hand—and the weapon—tangled up in the sheet and blanket. He began pounding at me with his other hand, his empty hand—his fist. Somehow I managed to hang onto the hand with the gun—and kept screaming."

"God," Peter said.

"I—I think the gun went off. It hardly made any sound, but I've got something like a deep scratch along my ribs—here." She touched the nightgown she was wearing. Along her left rib cage, Peter saw a thin streak of blood.

"Then you were there," Deborah said. "I tried to hang onto him but he managed to wrench free. Then—then you know the rest."

"Let me see," he said. He took her hand with the wet cloth in it away from her face. Her right eye was swollen shut. There was an ugly bruise on her jaw. If she hadn't taken that punishment and held onto the man's gun hand, they might both be dead, Peter thought.

She knew what had happened to Loomis. She'd heard his report on the red phone to the security people.

"Is it—is it very bad?" she asked.

"He's unconscious. His breathing's pretty thin. We can just pray he comes to and describes the man who attacked him," Peter said.

"He knew I was here—the man," Deborah said.

They had been so sure that nobody could know except Devery, Peter, and the police. Someone's foot had slipped, somehow, somewhere. Not the cops, not Peter, surely not Devery. So how?

Peter used the black phone again and called Devery at his apartment. The profanity that came over the line was unquotable.

The penthouse was presently swarming with people; Maxvil, Devery, half-a-dozen cops searching the rooftop, the stairway, the hall on the thirty-sixth floor for some clue. An ambulance crew had removed Loomis, and one of the young interns on the team was examining Deborah, who had managed to dress again during the wait for someone to come.

"You got lucky, lady," the doctor said. "That gunshot wound is just a scratch. An inch to the left and it could have gone right through your ticker. You'll just have to live with the facial bruises till they go away. Nothing broken."

In the mattress of Deborah's bed Maxvil's people found the bullet. The detective was certain it was from a .44 handgun. Ballistics would be able to tell whether it came from the same gun that had killed Gavin Hayes. None of them doubted that it would prove out.

The ambulance doctor reported that Loomis apparently had a fractured skull. No telling when—or if—he could talk.

Maxvil was as angry as Peter had ever seen him. His first target was Sergeant Croft, a late arrival. The sergeant's face was white and set marble-hard. Loomis was his friend and partner.

"So someone goofed," Maxvil said. "This murdering creep had no way of knowing Miss Wallace was here unless somebody's tongue wagged."

"I told Loomis what his assignment was," Croft said. "Also Cunningham, who's to take over at eight o'clock. You wanted them introduced to the lady and Mr. Styles, so there was no reason not to tell them in advance who they were guarding. But you know damn well, Lieutenant, neither of them would have done any talking."

"To someone else on the force?"

"These are two experienced policemen, Lieutenant, not some wild-eyed rookies. It was a secret assignment. They kept it secret, you can count on that."

Maxvil turned to Peter. "I'm not accusing you, friend, but did you talk to anyone—on the phone, perhaps—and let it slip that we were bringing Miss Wallace here?"

"You know I didn't," Peter said. "I made two phone calls from Miss Wallace's apartment. I called Devery and he made the suggestion that we bring Deborah here. Then I called you to get your approval."

"And you, Mr. Devery?" Maxvil asked.

"Not a soul," Devery said. "I made the arrangements myself without talking to anyone. That was after you called me to tell me to go ahead."

"I called you—" Maxvil eyes were narrowed, blazing with anger. "I called you on the switchboard phone. I didn't have another number for you. An operator could have listened in on that call."

"Surely you don't think—?"

"How else could it have leaked, if you're all telling the truth?" Maxvil said. "I want to talk to any operators who were on duty this afternoon when we talked."

You grab at any straw when there's nothing else, Peter thought. It was possible. An operator hears Deborah's name mentioned, a glamorous actress very much in the news because of two murders. Curiosity could have been too much for her. She listens. She passes it along to a friend, who passes it along to a friend. The word could have spread like a forest fire.

While the police and the building security people searched the premises for some sign of the killer, a decision had to be made about what to do with Deborah. It was Maxvil's view that she was safe where she was.

"We'll put on extra guards, of course," he said. "The fact that the man we're looking for knows where she is doesn't make it possible for him to get to her. We counted too much on secrecy. We'll count now on manpower. There's no way he can shoot himself past a half-a-dozen armed cops and get up that fire stair again. How do you feel about it, Miss Wallace?"

"If Peter will stay with me," she said. "I can't bear to be alone—anywhere."

"I have work to do," Peter said, "but I'll be right here in the building when I'm not with you."

"Who occupies the thirty-sixth floor, Mr. Devery?" Maxvil asked.

"There are six offices," Devery said. "Prize locations— light, airy, view of the whole city. Managing editor, chief editorial writer, our Washington editor, our entertainment department, a lady columnist who handles fashion and the like, our sports editor who writes a syndicated column."

"Can they be moved until this is over so that floor will be unoccupied?"

"The screams of outrage will be deafening," Devery said. "But, yes."

"The alternative is a cop in each office, body searches when people come and go. Somebody was on that floor with a murder weapon an hour ago. I don't want that gun getting that close to her again."

"I trust all those people, but I'll move them," Devery said.

"And get those switchboard operators to me," Maxvil said.

"What about the press in general?" Devery asked. "They'll be swarming over us, you know. There's not much chance this story won't leak. Too many people know it by now."

Maxvil swore softly. "Miss Wallace is not available for any kind of interview," he said. "No one except Peter is to get to her without my permission."

Devery's smile was grim. "The news people will think we're managing a scoop, with Peter, our best reporter, locked up here with her."

"I don't give a damn what they think," Maxvil said. "Peter is here helping me. If he writes one line about it without my say-so, I'll cut out his heart."

"I'm wondering if a full and detailed story isn't our best bet," Peter said. "Someone may have seen something, heard something. If they know what's happened here, they might come forward."

"Your magazine is a weekly," Maxvil said. "It comes out on Thursday. When does it go to press?"

"Tomorrow," Devery said.

"Write your story," Maxvil said to Peter. "I'll give you a stop or go on it at the last minute tomorrow—after I've seen it."

Devery took off to deal with the problem of the thirty-sixth floor. Croft joined the other cops in the search of the roof and the rest of the building for some sort of clue. A patrolman had taken the bullet found in the mattress to Ballistics to check it against the one that had been fired through Gavin Hayes's skull. Maxvil was left with Peter and Deborah.

"So, we'll do a hell of a fine job of locking the barn doors after the horse is gone," he said, still angry. "You'll be as safe here now, Miss Wallace, as if you were locked in a bank vault. But it's no thanks to us that you're still here to be protected."

"She deserves a medal for putting up such a fight," Peter said. "If she hadn't, we'd neither of us be here to talk about it."

Maxvil lit a cigarette and began to pace the room, restlessly. "It's another example of this creep's knowledge of layouts," he said. "He knew how to get in and out of your apartment, the Boswell Theater, and here. Damned systems of protection don't work. At seven o'clock they close up downstairs, night crew takes over. No one can enter the building without signing in and stating his business. But the guards have no way of knowing who's still in the building when they take over. Our man could have been here before seven o'clock and just waited for the right moment. Same way he handled things at the Boswell the night before. In before the night watchman started making his rounds. He knew the layout at Irving Place, at the theater, and here."

"But how did he get out?" Peter asked. "He had to pass the guards in the lobby to leave."

"So we can hope he hasn't left and that my men will find him," Maxvil said. "When several hundred people come to work this morning he'll just mingle with them and be gone, if we don't get lucky."

"But where can he hide?" Deborah asked, holding the wet cloth to her face.

Maxvil shrugged. "There are over two hundred offices in this building, plus storerooms, engine rooms in the basement, darkrooms where the magazine's photographers work, God knows what other places. It would take us a month to cover the whole territory. We have to get lucky."

"And if he knew how to get out as well as he knew how to get in, he could be in Cuba by now," Peter said.

"In a way I'd like to believe that," Maxvil said. "It would mean Miss Wallace is safe."

Deborah's violet eye, the one not covered by her compress, was opened wide. "You think he'll still try to get at me, Lieutenant?"

"He could try," Maxvil said. "He won't make it here. But as long as you don't remember what he thinks you know, you aren't going to be safe without an army surrounding you. For God's sake, woman, doesn't anything ring a bell with you?"

Deborah shook her head wearily from side to side. "I've tried and tried—"

There was a knock on the front door. It was Sergeant Croft, and with him were two young women. They looked scared out of their wits.

"The two operators who were on the switchboard when you made your call to Devery, Lieutenant," Croft said.

Peter knew them both, casually. Pamela Knight was a blonde, Maria Gonzales a dark, Spanish type. The Gonzales girl, he knew, spoke several languages and handled most overseas calls on her shift. He gave them a little wave of greeting.

"The lieutenant won't eat you, girls," he said.

The two girls had been routed out of their beds in their respective apartments by the police. They knew what had happened here in the penthouse. Croft had done a preliminary questioning.

"This one took your call, Lieutenant," Croft said, indicating Pamela Knight.

"You remember it?" Maxvil asked.

"Yes, sir." The Knight girl's voice was unsteady. "I answered the signal as always, 'Newsview Magazine.' You said, 'Mr. Devery, please.' I followed routine and asked who was calling. You said, 'Lieutenant Maxvil, police department, and it's an emergency.' I rang Mr. Devery's phone and told him you were calling. 'Put him on,' Mr. Devery said. I made the connection and heard Mr. Devery say, 'Hello, Lieutenant.' Then I got off the line. There were other calls."

"You didn't listen to any of the conversation?"

"No, sir. When the signal light showed me the call was over I disconnected."

"You mention the call to anyone?"

The Knight girl hesitated. "I spoke to Maria. She was sitting next to me at the switchboard. I told her the cop who was handling the Dale murder case was talking to the boss. 'Maybe there's a break in the case,' I said. Your name was all over the newspapers and the TV news, Lieutenant. I—I was a Bob Dale fan. I was naturally interested. But I didn't listen."

"You didn't know that Miss Wallace was being brought here to this penthouse?"

"How could I? I tell you, Lieutenant, I didn't listen to the conversation."

"Did you pass along to anyone else that I'd been talking to Mr. Devery?"

"I don't think so. I mean, I honestly don't remember that I did. And if I did, Lieutenant, it couldn't have been any big deal. The boss had been talking to the detective in charge of two murders. We're a newsmagazine, Lieutenant. There's nothing so unusual about Mr. Devery talking to someone involved in a big story. Happens all the time."

"Also," Maxvil said, his voice harsh, "if it became a

137

matter of record that you *had* listened in on my conversation with Devery you might very well lose your job. So why should you admit it?"

"There are calls and calls," the Gonzales girl said. She had a pleasant, low voice with a cultivated sound to her speech. "I cover most of the overseas calls from our various bureaus because I speak French, Italian, and Spanish. I am instructed to listen in so that there won't be any language problems. Pamela is also instructed to listen to the beginnings of any long-distance calls to make sure the connection is clear. But a local call—" She shrugged. "As soon as the caller is identified and the person it's meant for accepts it, she cuts out. The switchboard is a very busy place, Lieutenant."

Deborah took the compress away from her bruised face. It wasn't pretty to look at. "Somebody tried to kill me," she said. "He knew where I was and he came here to get me. How could he know I was here unless somebody passed on the information? I beg you, if you did tell someone, to tell Lieutenant Maxvil. It could save my life, Miss Knight."

Pamela Knight looked steadily at Deborah. "I didn't know you were here, Miss Wallace. I swear to you I didn't listen. I did tell Maria that the boss was talking to the detective in charge of the murders. I did wonder if there was some break in the case. I may have said that to someone else, but I don't remember that I did. If I did, it could only have been that the boss had had a call from the lieutenant. That was all I knew. I promise you."

"Everybody was talking about the murders," Maria Gonzales said. "I suppose every woman in the United States had a little bit of a crush on Bob Dale. He was as much of a public figure as the Kennedys. All yesterday afternoon people on the overseas calls asked me what I knew about it. But I didn't know that you were here, Miss Wallace, because Pamela didn't listen so she didn't tell me."

So much for one hopeful possibility. Peter was satisfied that the two girls were telling the truth. Listening in was not, after all, a serious crime. It went with the territory.

"If I had listened and heard that you were being brought here, Miss Wallace," Pamela Knight said, "I'd have known how important secrecy was. I wouldn't have told my own mother."

Maxvil showed his disappointment and also his belief that the two switchboard operators were on the level.

"Sorry to have routed you out of bed," he said. "I hoped you could help."

Sergeant Croft ushered the two girls out. Maxvil turned to Peter. "Does Devery have a private secretary?"

"His right arm," Peter said. "Sue Curtis."

"Does she work in the same office with him?"

Devery's office was in the heart of the newsroom. It was soundproofed against the noise of typewriters, phone conversations, people shouting back and forth to each other. Sue Curtis had her own office, adjoining Devery's, but not connected to it.

"But she would come and go without alerting him? Or could she pick up her switchboard phone and be in on his line?"

"No," Peter said. "As for her walking in and overhearing a conversation, let me say I think Devery would trust her with his life. As the Knight girl said, if Sue overheard only one end of the conversation she'd know how important secrecy was. She'd have discussed it with Frank. He'd have mentioned that to us."

Maxvil persisted. "A lot of people come and go to Devery's office?"

"There are probably fifty people working in that newsroom," Peter said. "Devery, in theory and in fact, is never shut away from anyone. You knock on his door and he invites you in."

"And if he didn't respond to the knock, you'd go away? Or would you open the door to see if he was there?"

"Could be, if you had just come in and didn't know for certain he was there. But if he was on the phone, you would back off."

"Unless you wanted to listen," Maxvil said.

"Frank's desk faces that door. If someone opened that door while he was on the phone, he'd see them. If the conversation was private, he'd wave them out. And once the door is closed you can't hear what's going on inside the office." Peter gave his friend a wry smile. "What about your end, Greg? Who could have heard what you were saying from your end?"

"When cops pass on secrets we've had the revolution," Maxvil said.

2

The red switchboard phone rang on the center table. Peter glanced at Maxvil, who gestured to him to answer.

"Is Mr. Styles there?" the switchboard operator asked.

"Speaking."

"A Mr. Cowley calling you, Mr. Styles."

Cowley, for God's sake, old Sam Cowley at The Players—the only Cowley Peter knew. "Hello, Sam," he said. "What can I do for you?"

"It's what I can do for you, Styles," the old man said, in his high, crotchety voice.

"So what can you do, Sam?"

"It's just possible I can provide you with an answer to all the horrors that are going on," the old man said.

"Well, Sam, the person for you to talk to is Lieutenant Maxvil. He's in charge of the case. He happens to be right here."

"No!" The old man's voice was sharp. "There are judgments to be made before I talk to the police. And you, Styles, are the only person who can make those judgments. Will you come and talk to me here?"

"Here is The Players? You're living there?"

"Yes."

Peter curbed his irritation. The boring old gossip couldn't have anything of real importance. He spent all his time at The Players bar and in the theatrical library there, reading his old plays and reliving his old successes.

"Sam, I don't think I can—"

"I tell you it's important, Styles."

"Hold on a minute." Peter covered the mouthpiece with his hand. "Our friend Sam Cowley," he said to Maxvil. "He thinks he's got something that might be helpful. Wants me to go down to The Players to talk to him. It can't be anything of any real consequence. Just some gossip he's picked up. He won't talk to you."

"Who knows?" Maxvil said. "We don't have a damn thing to go on; even gossip might be useful. But first I want you to come down to the newsroom and Devery's office with me. Someone down there may know how my phone call to Devery could have been overheard."

Peter looked at Deborah. "If I'm going to locate here with you, luv, I need some fresh clothes and my own razor and hairbrush. They're just around the corner from The Players at Irving Place. Probably take me a couple of hours to get down and back."

She looked frightened. "Peter, couldn't you—"

"You're absolutely safe here, Miss Wallace," Maxvil said. "I promise you. Cowley seemed to have a book full of information on Bob Dale. He may have remembered something—something that might help you to remember something."

Peter spoke into the phone again. "I can be there in an hour or so, Sam."

"It's ten minutes to eight," Cowley said. "I'll expect you by nine o'clock." The phone clicked off.

142

Deborah needed reassurance.

"You're surrounded by an army, luv," Peter said. "I've got to give Greg a guided tour of the newsroom. Then I'll be off downtown. It'll probably take old Sam an hour to tell me what could be told in five minutes. Then I'll pick up my stuff and head back here. What can I bring you? Caviar for lunch?"

She reached out to him. "Just bring yourself back as quickly as you can."

He bent down and kissed her unwounded cheek. *In the theater you always kiss hello and good-bye.*

The newsroom is on the second floor of the Newsview Building. It is a wide-open space with dozens of desks equipped with typewriters. The walls are lined with filing cabinets containing all manner of information valuable to writing reporters. There are four offices on the north wall: Devery's, a smaller one for Sue Curtis, his private secretary, and two for rewrite men who take phoned-in stories from reporters on the street and write them up for immediate use. There are telephones on every desk.

Even at eight o'clock in the morning half the desks were occupied, some reporters still there from the night shift, some just coming on for the new day.

Peter led Maxvil between the desks to the door of Devery's office and knocked. Devery was not alone. Max Lewis, the drama critic, wearing a bright pink linen suit, was with him. Even at eight o'clock in the morning Lewis was certain to be dressed in a style you couldn't forget.

"The gods must have been listening," Lewis said, as Peter and Maxvil entered. "I've been trying to get Frank to wangle me an interview with Deborah Wallace. I'm Max Lewis, Lieutenant. I'm doing a special feature on Bob Dale, and the Wallace woman has to know more about him than anyone else alive."

"I'm sorry," Maxvil said. "We're trying to get Miss Wallace to do some concentrating for us. I don't want her diverted."

"She hasn't come up with anything helpful?" Lewis asked.

Maxvil shrugged. "We haven't recognized it if she has."

Lewis gave Peter a sly look. "Is she as good in the hay, Peter, as one has been led to believe?"

"If I had time," Peter said, "I would wash out your mouth with soap."

"Well, I mean, old man, locked away with her for hours and hours—"

"How do you know that, Mr. Lewis?" Maxvil asked, sharply.

"The newsroom knows all, sees all," Lewis said. "The whole story of her being brought here last night, being shut away on the roof with Peter, the attack on her—it's all over the city by now."

"That's why I'm here," Maxvil said. "The killer knew last night, and the only way he could have known was by overhearing my conversation with you, Devery, on the telephone. I want to know how that was managed."

"The only thing I've thought about since the attack," Devery said. "How? I understand the switchboard girls came up clean."

"They seemed to be leveling with us," Maxvil said. "Tell me, Devery, if you wanted to hold a conference call, how would it be arranged? Suppose you wanted a reporter in the newsroom to be in on a conversation you were having with someone on the outside?"

"Series of complicated plug-ins at the switchboard," Devery said. "The switchboard girls wouldn't forget it. It's not routine. I can't remember ten times that it's happened, certainly not yesterday when I was talking to you."

144

"So you didn't give the orders, but could somebody have?"

"Not without an OK from me," Devery said.

"Excuse me if I leave you to unravel this little problem," Lewis said. "If I can't talk to Deborah Wallace, I've got to find someone else who knows Dale's life story. I was wondering about old Sam Cowley at The Players."

"If you want gossip and not facts," Peter said. "He just called me to say he may have the case solved."

"Oh, brother!" Lewis said. "Well, gentlemen, when it is possible to talk to Miss Wallace I'd appreciate your telling me. She's the only horse's mouth, I suspect."

The shocking pink evaporated through the door into the newsroom.

"If that bastard wasn't the best and most widely read drama critic in the city, I sometimes think I'd give him the boot," Devery said.

"I don't have time for office politics," Maxvil said. "I wondered about your secretary, Devery. Miss Curtis, is it?"

"Sue?"

"I understand you trust her. Peter called her your right arm. She could come and go without your paying any particular attention, couldn't she?"

"What are you getting at?"

"Could she have come into your office while you were talking to me? You wouldn't have noticed particularly, would you?"

"I wouldn't, only it didn't happen," Devery said. "I don't have any secrets from Sue, only she wasn't here to share one yesterday. Would you believe that yesterday Sue developed the first flaw I've ever detected in her? An infected wisdom tooth. She took the afternoon off to get it yanked."

"Someone knocked on your door when you were talking to me, opened the door. You waved him out, but not till he'd heard enough—?"

"It just didn't happen," Devery said.

"So we're barking up the wrong tree," Maxvil said. "There was an earlier call, Peter to you from Miss Wallace's apartment. That's when you first suggested bringing her here, right? Who overheard that conversation?"

Devery stared into space, looking back to the day before.

"I was in Sue's office when Peter called," he said finally. "Office next to mine." He gestured. "I went there to look for some proofs she'd neglected to bring to me before she went to the dentist. The tooth was driving her up the wall, so she wasn't her usual efficient self. When the switchboard couldn't reach me, they tried her. I answered the phone."

"And that was when you suggested to Peter that Miss Wallace would be safe here in the penthouse?"

"Yes. He was to call you and you were to call me back if you bought the idea."

"Miss Curtis's office isn't soundproofed like this, is it?"

Devery's face hardened. "Just partitions, halfway to the ceiling."

"So anyone in the newsroom who happened to be near that office could have heard everything you said."

Devery nodded slowly. "Yes, and it could have been any one of thirty or forty people."

"So let's get a list of them. We ought to be able to check 'em out by Columbus Day," Maxvil said bitterly.

It was a glimmer of light, but Peter understood Maxvil's frustration. From the very start, without any clue to motivation, he had been confronted by interminable lists of people who had been Bob Dale's friends, professional associates. The murder of Gavin Hayes had added names to

146

that list, facing them with interminable checking, both here in New York and in Hollywood. Now it could perhaps be narrowed, but there were still thirty or forty people, by Devery's estimate, to talk to, check out, cross-check. Maxvil had been known to call this "the ditch-digging of detective work." All your scientific know-how, your sophisticated computers, were useless when you were faced with the long, slogging business of question and answer.

"The newsroom is not exactly a private office," Devery said. "There are desks out there used by forty reporters. But you don't have to have a password to get in there. People involved in some story come in to talk to the reporter covering it. What I'm getting at is that in addition to the people who work out there, there could have been others."

"They wouldn't just be there sight-seeing," Maxvil said. "Your people would know who they were and why they were there, wouldn't they?"

"Each of my people would know who was there to see them, but they could see a stranger across the room and not know why he was there. What I'm trying to say is—"

"—that the killer could have just wandered into the newsroom and hung around, listening to the talk, listening to your phone conversation. Right?"

Devery nodded.

"So we dig," Maxvil said. He started away and turned back. "I can't duck the outside press much longer. They know Miss Wallace is up in the penthouse, that she was attacked. Do I tell them there are an army of cops up on the thirty-sixth floor, guarding the only way to the roof? Or do I tell them nothing except we're sure the killer won't try again?"

"I don't follow," Devery said.

"The killer will read what I say, or hear it on radio or TV. If he thinks we're being careless, he might make another try at it."

"You mean, invite him back?" Devery said. He looked shocked.

"You can't," Peter said. "You're always talking about the fact that you never get to investigate a crime till after its committed. You can't play games with Deborah's life."

"Oh, hell, of course I can't," Maxvil said. "It was just an idea. We'll advertise the army."

It was after nine thirty when Peter's taxi dropped him at The Players. The club is usually quiet at that time of day. There are only half-a-dozen bedrooms on the top floor, usually occupied by out-of-town members, occasionally by someone like old Sam Cowley who settled in for a longer stay. To Peter's knowledge Cowley was the only permanent resident, occupying the choice space at the top of the building called the penthouse, which was the only room with a private bath. The other rooms shared two baths on the fifth floor.

Breakfast was served in the bar for those few members in residence. Those few breakfasts were served by Dominic, an Italian waiter who had been with the club ever since Peter could remember.

"Mr. Cowley have breakfast about an hour ago," Dominic told Peter. "He go back upstairs, I think."

Peter took the creaking old elevator to the office on the fourth floor. He was always amused by a brass plaque in the elevator. It read, THE SARAH BERNHARDT ROOM. Legend had it that years ago, in the days of Stanford White, designer of the building, the Divine Sarah had been honored at the club and found herself stuck in this ancient monster.

148

The girl at the switchboard in the office rang Sam Cowley's rooftop quarters for Peter. There was no answer.

"Mr. Cowley spends a lot of time in the library," the girl told Peter.

Sam had mentioned the library. Peter walked down a flight of stairs. The Walter Hampden Memorial Library, repository for everything that has ever been written for and about the theater, plus programs and photographs of great stars of the past, was dark. Drapes still covered the windows, left drawn since last night. Peter remembered that the librarian didn't come in till ten o'clock.

He climbed back up the stairs and on to the fifth floor. From there, there was a narrow, winding stair to the roof. Peter had always thought that the penthouse was a firetrap. Smoke in that narrow, enclosed climb would have been impenetrable.

He reached the top and knocked on Sam's door. There was no answer. He tried the door; it wasn't locked. As he opened it he was instantly aware that the shower was running in the bathroom.

"Sam!" he called out.

The old man wasn't the neatest of men, Peter thought. There were clothes tossed around, bureau drawers standing open.

He went to the bathroom door and knocked. "Sam! It's Peter Styles!"

There was no answer. Damn the old idiot. As Peter opened the door, he was forced back by the cloud of steam. The hot water was running full blast in the shower stall. Strange the old boy should be taking a shower when he'd already been up, dressed, and had breakfast in the bar.

Almost before he pulled aside the curtain Peter realized there was trouble. The old man had passed out in the shower. He reached inside and turned off the water, almost scalding his hand and wrist.

Sam Cowley, fully clothed, lay on the floor of the shower stall. His glasses were still perched on his rabbitlike nose, but old Sam would never see through them again. The back of his head was smashed in, and blood swirled around, trying to find its way to the drain under his huddled body.

3

Peter stood staring down at the soaked and bloody remains of a once famous man. Does any man ever imagine that his end will come in this violent fashion? A little more than an hour ago old Sam Cowley had been his usual brisk and confident self. Come to me, I have answers. Peter hadn't really believed it, but he had come—too late. Someone else had believed.

He backed way from the shower stall and out into the room. He realized now that the disorder here was not simply old Sam's way of life. Someone had torn the room apart, looking for something. Whatever it was, had it been found?

There was a telephone on the side table beside the dismantled bed. The searcher had pulled off sheets and summer blanket, had obviously searched under the mattress because it was no longer resting squarely on the bed frame. Peter knew he should hesitate to handle the phone. He should go down to the office to make the necessary calls. But somehow he didn't want to leave old Sam alone in his bloody disaster. He took a handkerchief from his pocket, covered his hand, and dialed the office.

"Miss Watson? Peter Styles here. Mr. Cowley has had an accident," he said. "Will you send the club manager up here, please?"

"At once, Mr. Styles."

Then he dialed Devery's private line at *Newsview*.

"Frank? Peter. Somebody got to Sam Cowley before I did."

"Got to him?"

"Looks like more of the same. Head bashed in. Left, fully clothed, in a running showerbath in his room. Is Maxvil somewhere there?"

"He's outside in the newsroom. I'll get him."

As Peter waited he kept looking around the room. There had been no search like this at Irving Place when Bob Dale was killed, nor anything like it in Gavin Hayes's office at the Boswell Theater. There might be no relationship between this and the other crimes. Old Sam Cowley had made enough enemies with his incessant probing and gossip. But a gut feeling insisted that this was another part of one grisly pattern. Old Sam had stumbled on some crucial fact and died before he could pass it on.

Maxvil's harsh voice came over the line. "You called police headquarters?"

"I wanted to get to you first," Peter said. "It's surely all one ballgame."

"Good," Maxvil said. "I'll make the call. I can't be in three places at once. I want a man there I can work with. What's this about a showerbath?"

"He was slugged, pushed into the shower fully dressed, the hot water turned on."

"We're dealing with a lunatic!"

"Room searched, torn apart," Peter said. "He had to get

152

away. Not easy here at The Players. If the maid came to make up Cowley's room she'd hear the shower and go away. Delay any alarm.''

"Stay there till someone takes over," Maxvil said. "Try to keep helpful friends from messing up the joint.''

"Will do.''

Peter put down the phone. Footsteps were running up the outer stairway. Harmon, the club's professional manager, appeared in the open doorway.

"What's wrong, Mr. Styles?''

"Don't touch anything, but take a look in the shower," Peter said. "I've notified the police.''

Harmon, a middle-aged man wearing a neat, gray tropical-worsted suit, edged his way into the bathroom.

"Oh, Jesus!'' Peter heard him say.

Harmon backed out, turning to Peter. The color had drained from his face. "He had breakfast a little before eight. Dominic served him. He looked fine.''

"He called me about then," Peter said. "He thought he knew something that would help in the Dale and Hayes murders. He knew I was involved in those cases with the police. I came to hear what it was.''

"What can I do?" Harmon asked. "I suppose I should call Mr. Winters.''

Roland Winters, the actor, was president of The Players.

"First, check out on everybody who's been in the club since you saw Mr. Cowley at breakfast," Peter said. "Waiters, kitchen help, maintenance crew, maids, office staff, members. The police will want to know everyone who's come and gone this morning—may still be here.''

"Things are pretty quiet this time of day," Harmon said, "especially in summer. Only four of the bedrooms are occupied. There's no regular doorman or coatroom attendant. Everyone's busy cleaning up for the day. If someone

153

wanted to come in off the street, he might not be seen. Were you noticed when you came in, Mr. Styles?"

Peter realized he had not been noticed. He'd gone down into the bar and found Dominic clearing away the last of the breakfast dishes.

"Members don't begin to come in till a little before lunchtime, except those few who are living here," Harmon said.

"So it should be easy to make a checklist," Peter said. "I'll wait here for the police. Someone will have to show them up."

"I'll have a man on the door," Harmon said.

"Have him check on everyone who tries to go out," Peter said. "If there's a stranger, try to hang on to him."

"I'll put Usti on the door," Harmon said. "Nobody will get by him." Usti was a huge former fighter, cauliflower-eared, who was the head maintenance man.

Left alone, Peter walked over to the windows. Down below was Gramercy Park, lush green in the warm summer weather, surrounded by a high iron fence. Only residents of the area with keys could gain admission to the park. He could see the statue of Edwin Booth, great actor in the last half of the nineteenth century, who had given his home, this building, to his fellow actors and other professionals in the arts, as a club. Violence had been a tragic part of Booth's life, too. His brother, John Wilkes, had assassinated President Lincoln. Tragedy strikes from the most unexpected sources.

The damned shower was dripping, but Peter refused to go back into the bathroom and tighten it. He didn't want to look at Sam again unless he had to. The first shock of finding the old man was wearing off, and he found himself trying to put some facts together.

Sam had called him with the word that he had something

valuable to talk about. Maxvil and Deborah were present when the call came. They knew about it. Later on Devery and Max Lewis had heard about it. The only one after whose name he could place a question mark was the drama critic. Lewis had heard and wandered out of Devery's office. Forty minutes later Peter had headed for The Players. Lewis, in his pink suit, would have had only that much head start on Peter. Lewis was an arrogant ass. But a precision killer?

The word, Peter thought, that had cost Sam Cowley his life had almost certainly come from the old man himself. Sam had been a perpetual talking machine, determined to be important in every situation he encountered. He had been flattered when Peter and Maxvil had called him in as an "expert" on Robert Dale. The pièce de résistance would be if he could solve the crime for the police.

Peter could imagine the old man sitting in the bar the night before, surrounded by unwilling listeners, announcing that he had "something that might help the police solve the Dale case," titillating his audience by refusing to say what it was. Had something? Peter had assumed the old man had some bit of gossip about Dale, but as he looked around the room, which had been so thoroughly searched, he had to wonder if Sam had come into possession of some object, some physical clue.

Someone in Sam's audience had guessed what it was the old man had. Again, it could have been any one of dozens of members, or their guests, present last night. He waits for a chance to get to this room to search for—whatever. His moment doesn't come until Sam descends for breakfast this morning. While Sam is having his coffee and eggs the killer comes up here and begins to tear the room apart, looking for—whatever. Sam comes back too soon, having telephoned Peter. The killer has to kill in order to get away.

Farfetched? Maybe, maybe not. It would require another tedious bit of checking to determine who was in the club last night. And it might not be that at all. Sam could have talked to someone on the phone, someone he didn't suspect, and dangled the fascinating information that he had something that would solve the Dale case. One way or another, Sam had devised his own final curtain.

Outside on the street came the loud siren wail of an approaching police car. Maxvil hadn't wasted any time.

Sergeant Danvers, the Homicide man who followed Harmon, the club manager, up the narrow stair to Sam Cowley's room, was deceptively mild-mannered. Hatless, red-haired, with a kind of lopsided smile, he stood in the doorway, looking around the room.

"Mr. Styles? Greg Maxvil gave me a rundown on you. This the way you found it? I'm Sergeant Danvers." A pleasant voice, unruffled. You got the impression, somehow, that he knew what he was about.

"The body's in the bathroom, in the shower stall," Peter said.

Danvers didn't move, still surveying the room. "You touch anything? I understand you found him."

"I turned off the water in the shower before I realized what had happened. Place was full of steam. After that I used the phone, but I held it with my handkerchief."

There were voices on the stairway behind Danvers and Harmon. There was no way for Danvers's crew to crowd up into the room until the sergeant cleared the doorway. He didn't seem in a hurry.

"Any idea what someone was looking for?" Danvers asked.

Peter shook his head. "Maxvil probably told you that Cowley phoned me to say he had information that might be useful in the murder of Bob Dale. We supposed it was gossip. It looks as though it might have been something else."

"You can officially identify the body?"

"Samuel Cowley, a man in his eighties. He was a famous playwright thirty, forty years ago. Been a member of this club for half a century, I imagine."

"Elected in 1927," Harmon, the club manager, said.

"This his official address?"

"He has a small box downstairs in the bar," Harmon said. "He's been living here for about six weeks in this room. He has no other permanent residence that I know of. Travels around, visits friends in all parts of the country. We forward mail when he isn't staying here."

"I always hate to look at them," Danvers said, surprisingly. He crossed the room and went into the bathroom. The shower stopped dripping. After a moment or two he came back. "Is there some place we can talk? When my crew gets in here there won't be room to turn around."

"My office on the fourth floor," Harmon said.

Danvers went to the door. "OK, boys," he said.

A small army crowded into the room.

"Will you wait for me downstairs, Mr. Styles—and you, Harmon," Danvers said.

The usual routines of fingerprinting, photographing, and the medical examiner's preliminary work were about to begin. Peter and Harmon went down the two flights of stairs to Harmon's office. It adjoined the main business office. It was a plain, square room, windows overlooking adjoining rooftops, distinguished only by a collection of witty drawings by the famous caricaturist for *The New Yorker,* the late Al Frueh. There were sketches of Roland Young, Lionel Barrymore, Weber and Fields, Katharine Cornell, Bert Lahr, and others from the golden age of the twenties and thirties.

Peter sat down in a Windsor chair and for a moment

covered his face with his hands. The tensions had been so great for the last forty-eight hours that he found he was emotionally exhausted. Harmon had stopped off in the main office and now joined Peter.

"Here's a list of the people who have been in the club this morning," he said.

Peter glanced down the list. He knew most of the club's employees by their first names; the last names were unfamiliar. There had been only six members in the club, the list headed by Sam Cowley and himself. There had been an English actor playing in a Broadway show, the only other permanent resident. He was still asleep in his room on the fifth floor. Two other actors had been last-minute overnight guests. There had been a television star who had been on a late-night talk show. He had had breakfast at the same time Sam Cowley had been in the grill for his, and had left the club shortly after.

"There's always a chance there was someone else around who wasn't noticed," Harmon said. "As I told you, Mr. Styles, the regular coatroom attendant, the doorman, aren't on duty in the early morning. Someone could go to the elevator and get off at one of the upper floors without being seen. Librarian's only just arrived. People in the office aren't circulating."

"But maids, cleaning people?"

"None of them has added any names to this list," Harmon said.

Danvers came in from the outer hall. He glanced at the list. "We'll want to talk to all of them," he said. "The man who left the club after breakfast?"

"Easily reached," Harmon said. "He lives out in Quogue on the Island."

"See if you can contact him," Danvers said. "We'll start with the help. While you're getting them lined up for me,

158

Harmon, Mr. Styles and I will see what we can put together.''

Harmon took off.

Danvers sat down at Harmon's desk. He pulled a yellow legal pad in front of him and began to doodle on it. No questions. He was waiting for Peter to give.

"You know that Bob Dale was murdered in my apartment around the corner from here," Peter said.

Danvers nodded.

"I brought Maxvil here to talk to people who knew him," Peter said. "Sam Cowley was one of the first and most productive. He was a garrulous old guy, loaded with gossip about everyone in the theater. The theater was his life, you know. He wrote a dozen or more Broadway hits back in the days of these people." Peter gestured toward the Frueh drawings on the wall. "Those were great days, and Sam never tired of talking about them. He resented, I think, not being a part of the present. I think he spent most of his time trying to dig out gossip about the stars of today. He could tell us everything there was to know about Bob Dale's career, the plays he was in, the films he made, the television shows—and the women in his life.''

"Suggestions as to who might have killed Dale?" Danvers asked.

"Gavin Hayes, who was shot to death in his office at the Boswell Theater in the early hours of yesterday morning. That seems to have eliminated Hayes. Then early this morning there was an attempt to get at Deborah Wallace, who was Hayes's legal wife and Dale's current girlfriend.''

"Interesting triangle.''

"That's the name of the play Hayes and Dale were producing, with Miss Wallace in the cast—*Triangle*.''

"You could call it a family affair," Danvers said. "So this morning Cowley called you to say he had a lead?''

159

"He wouldn't talk to Maxvil," Peter said. "He told me there were 'judgments to be made' before he'd talk to the police."

"What did he mean by that?"

"No idea," Peter said. "Maxvil and I thought he probably just had some gossip of some sort; wanted to stay in the spotlight. But from the look of that room upstairs you have to think he had something concrete, some objects, a letter—something."

"Could have nothing to do with the Dale or the Hayes cases at all," Danvers said. "Old guy messing around with other people's secrets."

"That would be a pretty extraordinary coincidence," Peter said.

"We say we don't believe in them, but they happen," Danvers said. "Who might Cowley have talked to about this lead he had for you?"

"God knows," Peter said. "He was a tireless gabber, talk, talk, talk. I have a feeling he wouldn't have said what it was, but he could have hinted to dozens of people that he was cooperating with the police. It would have given him a special importance."

"He could have talked to people here in the club, or to friends somewhere else," Danvers said. "It isn't likely he'd have mentioned it to someone he suspected, is it?"

"The people he knew and might have boasted to are all theater people, all from the same world, you might say. They'd pass along what he might have said—they're all interested in the Dale case. Dale was a very popular guy. Sam could have talked here, or at Sardi's, or any one of half-a-dozen hangouts for theater people. What he had to say could easily have got back to the person he suspected without that person being around when he did his boasting. Maxvil said it. We're looking for a special needle in a haystack full of needles."

160

"Something a hell of a lot more solid than a needle," Danvers said. He was drawing some kind of a design on the legal pad. "I understand from Maxvil you actually had an encounter with the killer."

"Did he tell you that I have an artificial leg?"

Danvers nodded, not looking up.

"I woke up to the sound of Miss Wallace screaming," Peter said. "I don't remember, but I must have taken off the leg when I went to sleep. It's automatic, if you know what I mean. I reached for it, couldn't find it, and hopped, on one leg, into Miss Wallace's room. She'd tangled up his gun arm with her sheet and blanket and he was slugging at her with his left fist. I hopped toward him. He turned and took a swing at me. I was off-balance, no way to brace myself, and he knocked me flat. He took off out the window onto the roof. I couldn't follow."

"He didn't take a shot at either of you?"

"The gun went off in the tangle of sheet and blanket. The bullet just skimmed Miss Wallace's rib cage and buried itself in the mattress."

"But he still had the gun?"

Peter nodded.

"I wonder why he didn't use it," Danvers said. "If he came there to silence Miss Wallace, why not? He'd knocked you down. He had plenty of time to polish her off if that was his intention. Both of you, for that matter."

Peter shook his head slowly. "There was no question that he meant to kill Bob Dale," he said. "There was no apparent search of my apartment. Dale must have been asleep because he put up no kind of fight, and he was an athletic, vigorous man. The killer went there to kill. In Gavin Hayes's case he was shot in cold blood while he worked at his desk. No struggle, no search. If the killer was following the same pattern, he could easily have killed Deborah before she ever got him tangled up in that blanket and sheet.

And, as you say, he could have managed it after he got free and had disposed of me."

"But he didn't," Danvers said.

"Now you have old Sam upstairs. This time, the big search for something. You have to think that killing Sam wasn't his primary plan. The old man caught him in the act of searching."

"And Cowley knew who he was," Danvers said. He drew a jagged line on his legal pad. "So we have a killer who kills twice, in cold blood, for a reason we haven't uncovered. Then—if it's the same man and the same case—he tries twice to get at Miss Wallace, but doesn't take the opportunity he had to kill her. And—if it's the same man and the same case—he searches Sam Cowley's room and kills the old man when he's caught in the act."

"It has to be the same man and the same case," Peter said. "Deborah Wallace was the closest person in the world to Dale and Hayes. And Sam Cowley was trumpeting to the world that he might have the solution to the Dale case. For my money there's no question that all four violences are linked together."

"I guess it would be stubborn of me not to buy that," Danvers said. "Which leads us to think something else. There is some object, some physical clue, that would tell us who the killer is. He searched for it upstairs here. Perhaps he thought Miss Wallace had it and it was his plan to force her to hand it over."

"She doesn't have anything," Peter said. "If she has, she doesn't know what it is or that she has it."

"But this morning, after your call from Cowley—which our boy gets wind of in some fashion—he thinks what he's looking for may be here and not with Miss Wallace."

"Did he find it?"

Danvers shrugged. "Not at first, certainly. He searched

every drawer, every nook and cranny of that room, even the bed clothes and the mattress. It took him a hell of a lot longer than he hoped, which is why he got caught. Maybe he found it in the end. More likely, he didn't." The detective grinned at Peter. " 'Is it smaller than a breadbox'—the old twenty-questions gambit. It's not something bulky, for sure, or he wouldn't have been looking under the mattress."

"So where do we go from here?" Peter said.

"Fingerprints, whatever may give us a lead," Danvers said. "I'm not hopeful. There weren't any in the other cases that I know of. But if I were Maxvil—and I'll suggest it to him—I'd really turn the heat on the switchboard system at *Newsview*. Someone knew you were bringing Miss Wallace there. Someone may have overheard Cowley's call to you. How else would the man know?"

"Sam shooting off his mouth in the club last night, talking to someone on the phone from here."

"So we'll find out if he made any calls. We'll find out who was around last night when—and if—he was boasting. Meanwhile," and Danvers's voice hardened, "we have a maniac running around loose, armed, we have to think, with a .44-caliber handgun, ready to kill anyone who gets in the way of his finding something that could be hidden under the mattress of a bed. That suggests that you, and I, and Maxvil, and an army of cops are all clay pigeons in a shooting gallery. He'll take a pop at anyone who gets in the way of finding what he's looking for."

"He must know he can't go on forever without getting caught," Peter said.

Danvers stood up. "When a psycho like this runs amok you can't assume that he thinks rationally about anything. The first two killings—Dale and Hayes—smell like revenge of some sort. No search for anything in either case, just plain, vicious murder. Then he starts looking for something, doesn't kill Miss Wallace or you when he has the chance, kills Cowley only because he got caught searching."

"There is an actor named Smallwood—"

"I know," Danvers interrupted. "Maxvil told me. He couldn't have made the first attempt to get at Miss Wallace. You and Maxvil were with him. All he needs is an alibi in one of these situations to be cleared in all of them." He shook his head. "Unless we're dealing with a gang."

The phone on Harmon's desk rang. Danvers answered. "Yes, Lieutenant. No, nothing yet." A longish hold while he listened. He swore, softly. "I'll keep in touch. Let you know anything we find." He put down the phone and looked at Peter, his blue eyes suddenly cold as two newly minted dimes. "Maxvil," he said. "Sergeant Loomis, the cop who was guarding the fire stairs at *Newsview*, died without ever talking. So the sonofabitch has killed four times. I want him so bad, Mr. Styles, I can taste him!"

Peter had promised to get back to Deborah Wallace as quickly as he could. He'd estimated a couple of hours. The drama at The Players had stretched that time considerably. Now, as he walked out into the bright, late morning sunshine beating down on the park and the lonely statue of Mr. Booth, he had an almost irresistible urge to throw in the towel, to get away from the whole bloody insanity. The case was in the hands of highly competent professionals, Maxvil, Danvers, and their crews. Bob Dale and Gavin Hayes had meant almost nothing to Peter; names he knew, personalities he had encountered very briefly. Old Sam Cowley was not someone for whom he'd felt any warmth. He'd spent most of the years he'd known Cowley avoiding the old man's interminable reminiscences. He wouldn't have to hear them anymore.

Deborah Wallace, a frightened glamour package, had aroused some phony, boyhood gallantry in him. Sir Peter, the White Knight, protecting a damsel in distress. He had been dragged away from his cottage in the country, dragged away from the attempt to rehabilitate himself from his personal shocks and wounds. He had nothing to contribute to the solution of these murders. He wasn't a policeman, he was only an observer, a reporter.

That, damn it, was the trouble. It was his story. He had to see it through to the end. He thought of Wilfred Joyce, the Professor, downtown in Maxvil's office, moving his little wooden blocks around. He should be just that impersonal himself. Joyce saw Dale, and Hayes, and Deborah, and now old Sam Cowley, as bloodless little wooden blocks to be moved into the right positions so that they made a picture. Peter knew he should look at the puzzle in just that fashion.

He glanced across the park to where there was a taxi stand just outside the hotel there. He could walk over there, take a cab to the garage where he kept his car, and head back for the cottage in the Berkshires. For almost fifteen years now his personal and professional life had been surrounded by an endless stream of violence. He'd had enough. He didn't want an hour more of it. Yet, when he began to walk, he found himself headed in the wrong direction, headed for his apartment on Irving Place. He hadn't sold himself. He was going to get himself some fresh clothes, a razor, a hairbrush, other necessities, and go back to the *Newsview Building* and "the damsel in distress." He would stick this one out to the end, but never again.

He knew, as he walked, that he was lying to himself. This was his life, not as he had planned it, but as it was. He was stuck with himself.

Some kids were playing stickball in the street outside his

apartment building. He paused to watch them for a minute or two. Anything to avoid going back into action. Finally he went into the house, unlocked his front door, and stepped into the apartment.

He stopped dead in his tracks on the little raised vestibule that led into his living room. Sitting in the high-backed, overstuffed armchair that he thought of as "my chair" was Max Lewis in his gaudy pink suit.

"Welcome home," Lewis said, grinning at him.

"How the hell did you get in here?" Peter asked.

"Like Kipling's elephant child," Lewis said. "I wanted to see how it was done. Came over the garden fence. My insatiable curiosity."

Peter felt an unreasoning outrage at this invasion of his privacy.

"So what do you want?" he asked, his voice cold.

"I went down to The Players to see Sam Cowley," Lewis said. "You remember? You suggested it. Usti was on the front door and he told me what had happened. You found Sam, he said."

"Yes."

"God, what a shocker it must have been for you." Lewis fished a cigarette out of his pocket and lit it with a gold lighter. "This has become more than just an article on Bob Dale's career for me. I mean, one's curiosity gets unbearable."

Peter's impulse was to throw this arrogant bastard out on his ear. Reason told him that he could answer a few questions and get rid of him faster than by starting a brawl.

"Someone was searching Sam's room while he had breakfast," he said. "Sam must have caught him at it and got himself killed."

"Did the someone find what he was looking for?" Lewis asked. His eyes were bright with excitement.

"No way to tell," Peter said, "because the cops don't have any idea what he was looking for."

"And you don't?"

"No. How should I?"

"Because you're a very bright boy, Peter. I thought perhaps the Wallace dame might have suggested something that would give you an idea."

"Nothing."

"Sam, when he talked to you, asked you to come see him, didn't give you a clue?"

"No."

Lewis stirred restlessly in the big chair. The ash from his cigarette dribbled down the front of his pink suit. He seemed not to notice. "No idea what Sam had that would have pointed to Dale's killer?" he asked.

"None. And now, if you'll excuse me, I've got to gather up some clothes and head uptown. The police haven't got far enough at The Players to have produced anything positive." Peter started for the bedroom door.

"Have you mentioned to anyone that I was looking for the manuscript of a play here yesterday?" Lewis asked.

Peter turned. The man's voice seemed high and tense.

"I don't think so. Why? Is that important?"

"It will surface sooner or later," Lewis said. "You'll tell someone and they'll add it up." He made a choking sound as he uncoiled and stood up. "You see, that's what I was looking for in Sam's room."

Peter felt the blood in his veins turn to icewater. "*You?*" he said.

"I'm afraid so, Peter. And I just can't let you pass it on."

Lewis's hand came out of the pocket of his pink coat, and Peter found himself staring into the barrel of a very efficient-looking handgun.

4

The business of investigating a crime hadn't turned out to be exactly what Greg Maxvil had imagined it would be when he had gone into training at the police academy years ago. All the scientific aids were there as advertised. Ballistics was there for the identification of weapons; millions of Americans had been fingerprinted and were on file. The magic of the laboratory could classify bloodstains by type; analyze urine, semen, the food contents of a stomach; detect the presence of poisons, of disease. Cameras permanently recorded the scene of a crime that had to be dismantled so that life could go on. Computers organized facts, produced matching patterns, answered questions in seconds that it would take a man hours to unearth. All the promised scientific help was there, but nine times out of ten—unless it was a family quarrel, or a brawl in a bar, or the criminal was stupid or careless—the solution came down to the answer to one simple question: Why? The classic answers were money, revenge, jealousy. Or to label them differently, greed, hatred, a woman.

It had been more than forty-eight hours since this particular chain of violence had begun with the bludgeoning to death of Bob Dale. There were now four murders, including that of Sergeant Loomis, who had simply been an obstacle in the killer's path, not a part of his pattern. The scientific forces had been unleashed and they had, so far, produced almost nothing. Item: the bullet that had killed Gavin Hayes and the bullet that had been fired at Deborah Wallace. Science determined that both bullets had been fired from the same .44-caliber handgun. But there was no record of any other bullet fired by that gun in the police files or the FBI files. Item: traces of oil had been found in Bob Dale's crushed skull, suggesting that he had been beaten to death with the butt of a gun. Probably the same gun.

Probably. Possibly.

And there the armaments of science had broken down. No fingerprints that couldn't be accounted for; no piece of cloth, no mysterious hair, no tobacco ash—none of the things that delight the hearts of crime writers.

Motive, the why of it; that's what Maxvil faced, and without any leads that went anywhere. In the beginning Gavin Hayes had looked promising as a suspect; a quarrel over a woman, money disagreements in a business relationship, the hint of some kind of blackmail by Dale years ago. Then Hayes is murdered and turns out to be no suspect at all. Lucien Smallwood, the disgruntled actor fired from his job by both men—Dale and Hayes. But Smallwood couldn't have made the attempt to get into Deborah Wallace's apartment. He had been with Maxvil and Peter at the time. He couldn't have broken into the *Newsview* penthouse or attacked Sam Cowley at The Players. He had been under surveillance when those things happened and was accounted for around the clock.

Why?

The answer to that why was lying around somewhere for Maxvil to find, buried in someone's reluctant memory, hidden in some business transaction, cloaked by some apparently trivial wrong done to someone, clouded over by scores of love affairs in which Bob Dale had been involved. Money, revenge, jealousy. But which?

Downtown, Wilfred Joyce, the Professor, moved his wooden blocks around and came up empty.

About noon of this third day Maxvil had sought out privacy for himself. He needed the chance for some concentrated thinking, without interruptions from his own staff, from the media, from anxious friends of the victims. He needed a chance to search for that elusive why. The office belonging to the sports columnist on the thirty-sixth floor was the place he chose. Devery had emptied all the offices on that floor. It was a pleasant, sunny room, windows looking out toward the river, the walls covered with photographs of famous sports figures, autographed for the columnist. What a break it must be, Maxvil thought, to deal with violent conflicts that were all ended by the clock—the end of the game, the end of a round, the end of an inning or a period, all controlled by rules. A psychotic killer played by no rules, his violence came to no predetermined conclusion.

Why? Goddamn it, *why?*

Maxvil had been wrestling with that question for about half an hour when someone knocked on the office door. Damn it, he had given orders—

It was Sergeant Croft. "I'm sorry, Lieutenant," the sergeant said, "but Robert Dale's lawyer is here from Hollywood. Just came in from Kennedy. I thought you'd want to know."

"Where is he?"

"Right here with me, Lieutenant. Mr. Martin Farraday."

Maxvil let out his breath in a long sigh. "Come in, Mr. Farraday," he said.

The lawyer was a man in his forties, Maxvil guessed, sun-tanned, athletic-looking, wearing a seersucker suit with a navy-blue sports shirt, open at the throat. He was carrying an expensive-looking brief case. His smile was tentative, but white enough for a toothpaste ad.

"Sorry if I'm interrupting," he said.

"If you've got anything helpful, you're welcome," Maxvil said. "If you haven't, I'll very quickly kick you out on your behind."

The lawyer sat down across the desk from Maxvil, putting the cowhide briefcase down in front of him. "I don't know what I have," he said. "But all there is to know about Bob Dale's affairs, including his will. I'm a little too much in shock Lieutenant, to evaluate what I've got."

"Have you been brought up to date?"

"Taxi, coming in from Kennedy. The driver had his radio on and was talkative. I knew about Gavin, of course. Incidentally, he was my client, too. Now I've heard that Sam Cowley, the old playwright, is dead and that the police connect it with the other two. I'm not sure I understand why."

Maxvil explained about Cowley's call to Peter with the word that he had something that might help solve the Dale case. "Styles found him dead when he got there. So far Homicide hasn't come up with anything brilliant."

"It just doesn't make any sense," Farraday said.

"That's why I was shut away here," Maxvil said, "trying to make sense out of it, why I'm not interested in small talk about it." He lit one of his innumerable cigarettes. "Maybe it isn't sensible to try to make sense out of psychotic behavior. You know Deborah Wallace?"

"Of course. Well. There was a time when she and Bob—"

"That time had been renewed with the current play. She

172

was with Dale a short time before he was killed. She had a television show in the morning or she might have been there when the killer struck.''

"God! Where is she?''

"Here in this building, being guarded by an army. The killer tried to get at her, too—twice.''

"It's lunatic!'' Farraday said.

"You mentioned a will,'' Maxvil said.

Farraday tapped the briefcase on the desk. "A copy here. It's a reasonably complicated document, but I think I know what interests you. Who benefits by his death?''

"Who?''

"Nobody,'' Farraday said. "That is to say, no one individual. Bob had accumulated quite a little nestegg, you know. Made about a hundred grand a week on that 'Casanova Smith' thing for eight years! He had no ex-wives, no children.'' The corner of Farraday's mouth twitched. "No children that he was aware of. God knows he could have had dozens. What a man! But he had no legal heirs. I'd guess he's left a couple of million bucks. There are some odd bequests—like his estate will buy all the drinks for a day at The Players, big party in Hollywood for all the regulars on 'Casanova Smith.' There's a small bequest—five grand—to a couple who kept house for him in Hollywood. But the bulk of it is split between the old actors' home in Hollywood and the one here in the East—I think it's in New Jersey. So you see, no single person profits by his death. The fact is, a lot of people lose by it. He was box office. He would have made a lot of money for a lot of people over the next years, provided jobs for many more.''

"Legal problems? Law suits?''

Farraday shook his head. "He wasn't a quarreler. He had a couple of foul-ups with some sharpshooters out on the

Coast, might have brought suit against them. I advised him to. He just laughed me off. He didn't have time or interest in legal wrangling. These were violations of contracts where he might have picked up a few bucks. But he was rolling in money so he didn't give a damn.''

"Nobody he punished or damaged by some action of his?"

"Not that I know of."

"There was an actor here." Maxvil told the lawyer about Lucien Smallwood.

"He was a stickler for strict professionalism," Farraday said. "I suppose a few people lost jobs along the way because his standards were so high. But I never heard any big hullaboo about anything."

Maxvil inhaled on his cigarette. "So money doesn't seem to have been the motive. You were his lawyer. Didn't he have an agent?"

Farraday nodded. "Dick Wexler. He's one of the best. He's in London and called me from overseas. It's a blow for him. Bob's commissions were keeping him in caviar. Of course there'll still be residuals from the TV show for a long time."

"So that's all you've got, Mr. Farraday?"

"I'm afraid so," the lawyer said. "It does eliminate a search for someone who's going to get rich from it, doesn't it?" When Maxvil didn't answer he stood up. "Is there any reason why I can't see Deborah? She'd think it strange if I didn't look her up."

"If you don't mind company," Maxvil said. "There are two cops in the apartment with her."

"What a thing for her—both Bob and Gavin."

Maxvil picked up the phone and asked for the penthouse. One of his men answered and put Deborah on the line.

"Mr. Farraday is here. Asks to see you," Maxvil said.

"Martin? But of course—if it's all right with you."

"I told him it wouldn't be very private."

"That doesn't matter. Lieutenant?"

"Yes?"

"What has happened to Peter? He'd been much longer than he expected."

"He didn't expect to find a dead man," Maxvil said, sharply.

"He's with the police there?"

"I assume so," Maxvil said and put down the phone. Farraday was at the door.

"There's something I meant to tell you, Lieutenant. It's probably nothing. The last time I heard from Bob was about five days ago. He called me on the Coast and asked me what I knew about the laws of plagiarism."

"Plagiarism?"

"Literary theft," Farraday said.

"That's what he called you for? He didn't just ask you that in passing?"

"That's what he called for. I'm not a literary lawyer. I told him I'd get some facts for him and call him back. He said not to break my neck, there was no great hurry."

"And did you get back to him?"

"No. Something important came up and I didn't get around to it. Then, two days later, the news came about his death."

Maxvil punched out his cigarette in the metal ashtray on the desk. "Was Dale a writer among his other talents?" he asked.

"As far as I know he never wrote a line. Oh, I suppose he worked with the writers on his films, his TV shows, his plays. But, as far as I know, he never wrote anything original."

"So who was stealing from who?" Maxvil asked.

"Search me," Farraday said.

5

Peter stared, not believing, at the gun that was leveled straight at his chest, then raised his eyes to look at what was obviously a madman. Max Lewis's familiar face was somehow twisted almost out of recognition. The dark eyes were bright, as if fires burned behind them. The sardonic smile, a trademark of Max Lewis, the sophisticated drama critic and man-about-town, had become a thin, sadistic slit. Peter knew, without being warned, that he was a finger-twitch away from being dead. Say the wrong thing, ignite the killer impulse in this man he'd thought he knew so well, and his participation in this world's affairs was only a fraction of a second away from being finished.

"You look surprised, Peter," Lewis said. His tensions created an excitement that made his voice unsteady.

"To put it mildly," Peter said.

Long ago, in an apartment thirty stories above the street, Peter had stood in the shadows behind a skillful cop who was trying to talk a potential suicide in off the window ledge. One wrong gesture, one wrong word, and the man on the ledge would have hurtled through space to the street below. In the end the cop, after an hour of talk, held out his hand and helped the man in.

"You keep 'em interested, away from their preoccupation with dying," the cop had told Peter afterwards. "Maybe someone will get to them from above, or below, while you keep 'em talking. The main thing is not to anger them, seem interested in their problem whatever it is, ask about it, sympathize with it."

Peter knew that he was, in effect, high up on that ledge and about to be shoved. No one would be trying to get to him from "above or below." His one remote chance was to persuade Lewis to talk about what had driven him to this. While they talked it was possible Peter would find a way to get at the man, get at the gun.

He found it difficult to keep his eyes off the gun—the finger inside the trigger guard which had only to contract ever so slightly to end all this—and make direct eye contact with Lewis.

"If you were looking for your playscript in Sam's room, you must have been the person who slugged him and left him in the shower," Peter said.

"Miserable old creep," Lewis said. "He was eating breakfast when I got to the club. I thought I'd have time."

"I tipped you off to the fact that he might have it?"

"It made sense. Dale might have passed it on to him."

"Or Gavin Hayes?"

"Oh, I knew Gavin didn't have it," Lewis said. "But he knew about it. Dale told him. They both threatened me."

"I don't understand, Max. Threatened you with what?" Peter fought to keep himself looking straight at the man and not at the gun.

"Long story. There's no time for long stories, is there, Peter?"

Peter forced an artificial smile. "I have time, Max. All the time in the world."

178

"Sorry, Peter."

"You did kill Dale and Hayes?" Peter asked. He could feel a trickle of cold sweat running down his back, inside his shirt.

"Yes. And I'm very good with this gun, Peter. I shot Hayes from fifteen feet away, right between the eyes."

"A four-year-old child couldn't miss me from where you're standing now," Peter said. "Relax, man. Surely you won't refuse to satisfy my curiosity before you pull that trigger. You tried to get at Deborah Wallace, too?"

"I needed to talk to her and, I thought, to you. Someone might have let slip where that playscript is. Dale might have told the whole story to Deborah, and she could have passed it on to you. I've got to find that goddamned script."

"You didn't look for it when you killed Dale. This apartment wasn't searched—not like Sam's room."

"Dale told me it wasn't there," Lewis said. " 'Don't bother to break into my apartment to look for it,' he told me. 'I've got it stashed away where you won't find it.' "

"But you killed him anyway. How did you get in here that night?"

"Over the back fence, into the garden. I knew Deborah would be leaving him because she had a TV show. I waited for her to go, and gave him a little time to get to sleep. Hell, Peter, you didn't know I once had an apartment two houses down the block, did you? I knew the backyard geography well."

"And you knew the backstage at the Boswell Theater well too, didn't you? Probably been there often, visiting, interviewing."

"Dozens of times," Lewis said.

"So you slipped in there and waited for Hayes to come back for some late-night work."

"I thought the sonofabitch would never come," Lewis said. "But he came. And he laughed at me." A nerve twitched high up on Lewis's cheek. "It didn't make any real difference that he laughted at me. It just made it quicker."

Every bone in Peter's body ached. He hadn't moved a muscle since Lewis had produced his gun. He reached out for the door jamb, shifted his weight, felt relief. He saw Lewis's eyes narrow and guessed that the finger in the trigger guard had tightened ever so slightly. *Seem interested in their problem whatever it is, ask about it, sympathize with it.*

"Dale and Hayes must have really put the screws to you to earn what you gave them," Peter said.

"Dale was a self-righteous bastard. Hayes had all the meanness of the queen he was," Lewis said. "Always eager to slip a knife between your ribs. Well, he saw it coming, anyway. I saw the fear in his eyes. I didn't have that pleasure with Dale. Couldn't risk it with him. Athletic hero! He might just have got away from me if I'd waked him so he'd know he was paying for being a bastard."

"Those are the first negative comments about Dale anyone has given me in the last couple of days," Peter said.

"You haven't talked to the right people" Lewis said. "All that crap about how professional he was. He was a man without morals. Ask a hundred guys whose women he stole. But I must live my life according to his rules! Jerk of the first order!"

"How could he tell you how to live your life?" Peter asked.

Lewis's smoldering eyes narrowed. Wrong question, Peter thought, touching on the wrong nerve. He changed directions, quickly.

"You gave Dale an enthusiastic review in *Triangle*," he said.

"You can be a jerk of the first order and still be a fine

actor," Lewis said. "The name of the game, you might almost say. Actors aren't like ordinary people; vain, self-important, ego-ridden. I don't review an actor's performance on the basis of what I know about him as a human being."

"Some people think you can be very cruel when you're taking an actor or a play apart."

"My style," Lewis said. "Ask Frank Devery. Like it or not, it gets readers. If I tear an actor apart in print, you can hear him howling all around Sardi's and The Players that I have some kind of personal grudge against him. His ego won't let him accept the possibility that I could be right about his giving a lousy performance. Theater people, by and large, actors, writers, producers are all the same breed of cat. They won't admit to a bad performance, a bad play, a fault in judgment. Would you believe that Jake Goldman once barred me from all the Goldman-owned theaters for six months because I lambasted a turkey in which he'd invested his own money? The critic is the enemy of anyone he criticizes."

Keep him singing his own tune, Peter thought.

"I guess writers sometimes have the same feeling about editors," he said.

"They shouldn't—not about good editors. Theater people shouldn't feel it about good critics. I'm a good critic, the best in the business. There hasn't been anybody as good since Brooks Atkinson stopped writing for the *Times*."

"You lower the boom a lot more cruelly than Atkinson ever did," Peter said.

"It's a different age, different readers," Lewis said. "Today's reader wants to be amused as well as informed. Theater people set themselves up to be knocked down, like pins in a bowling alley. They walk out on stage to be shot at. If they're good, they survive. If they stink, they quite properly get gunned down. It isn't the critic's job to be a sympathetic undertaker."

"You didn't shoot down *Triangle,* or Dale's performance in it, or Gavin Hayes's direction of it. You praised the play, the performances, the direction."

"Because the play was good, the performances—especially Dale's and Deborah Wallace's—excellent, the direction superb. I reported what I saw that opening night."

"So nobody in that setup was throwing rocks at you after your review appeared."

"Oh, they were all delighted with me for a change," Lewis said, the nerve in his cheek twitching again. "So why—what has happened? Is that what you want to ask me, Peter?"

"More than that, I want to ask you if I can get myself a cigarette," Peter said.

"Where are they?"

"In a box on the table behind you there in the living room."

Anything can change this direct confrontation. Any kind of rearrangements of their positions could relax things.

Lewis took a step backward and to the right, the gun still aimed steadily at Peter. "Help yourself," he said. "And don't imagine that any kind of heroics will change things, Peter."

The gun was too ready, the intention behind those dark, hot eyes too clear, to try anything. But moving ten feet to the table was a blessed relief. For a moment Peter's back was turned to Lewis, and he wondered, as he opened the silver box on the table, whether that was the way he would get it—in the back!

He took a cigarette out of the box, lit it with his lighter, marveled at how steady his hands were. He turned, slowly, exhaling smoke. Lewis hadn't moved, the gun was still carefully aimed. Peter was only a foot or two further away from that pointed barrel than he had been in the doorway. *I shot Hayes from fifteen feet away, right between the eyes.*

"Peter, I admire you," Lewis said. "I've always admired you. Top man at your job. I regret this. I regret it very much. But I don't have any choice. You see, I don't intend to be caught, so there is no way I can let you go."

The telephone on the table started to ring. Instinctively, Peter reached for it.

"Peter!" Lewis's voice was loud, harsh. "Let it ring. Let it ring, Peter."

It rang six or seven times. The caller was hopeful of an answer. The room was still again except for Lewis's rather heavy breathing.

6

The endless routines of checking lists of names, assessing the nonproductive reports from the fingerprint men, photographers, and medical examiner's office, and inching not one step closer to a solid lead had Lieutenant Maxvil up the wall. In some cases you know very little about the victims of a crime, which makes it hard to get a glimmer of motive—the why that obsessed the detective. In this case books could be written about the victims, with the exception of the unfortunate Sergeant Loomis, killed in the line of duty. Thousands of people had wisps of gossip to offer about a great film, TV, and stage star like Bob Dale. A whole other generation of oldsters was ready to talk about Sam Cowley, a writer for the stage who had rubbed elbows in his time with such greats as George S. Kaufman, Marc Connelly, Philip Barry, Maxwell Anderson. Gavin Hayes had been called the boy wonder, rivaling the earlier Jed Harris for that title. You could sit back, Maxvil thought, and listen to thousands of fascinating ancedotes about the three dead men until Christmas. But in all that talk being heard today on radio and TV and crowding the newest Middle East crisis off the pages of the newspapers, where was the one sentence, the one inadvertent reference, that would point a finger at the psychotic killer?

Maxvil was tired of hearing about "the time when Bob Dale . . . ," "the night when old Sam Cowley . . . ," "the row Gavin Hayes had with the late Clark Gable . . ." What about three days ago, four days ago? What had set a sick mind onto a murder course? The motive, Maxvil told himself, didn't lie in legends of the past. Something very recent, he felt certain, had driven a madman off his rocker. Where to find it?

The murderer had been active in five different locations: Peter's apartment on Irving Place, the Boswell Theater, Deborah Wallace's apartment on Thirty-eighth Street, the penthouse on the roof of the Newsview Building, and finally, The Players on Gramercy Park.

Sergeant Burke had checked out the Irving Place area. No one had seen or heard anything unusual there, no tenants in the building itself or the surrounding buildings. How could you expect anyone to be looking out at those rear gardens at two in the morning? Bob Dale's killer wouldn't have arrived to a fanfare of trumpets. Dale had occupied Peter's apartment for only a few days. He'd given a house-warming party for the people in the *Triangle* company, and Deborah Wallace had visited him there. But Dale hadn't been in residence long enough for Irving Place to have become the center of his life.

The Boswell Theater had been the hub of activity for both Dale and Hayes for the last weeks. Six nights and two matinees, eight performances a week, plus previews before the official opening. Dale's dressing room at the theater had been set up as a place to receive, to live the major part of his life if he so chose. Unlike the rather bare spaces occupied by the other actors—dressing table, lighted mirror, a couple of straight chairs—Dale's room had a couch, where he could rest between matinee and evening performances, or do whatever else a man like Bob Dale might do on a couch; a refrigerator with an ice-making machine; a teakwood cabinet that the prop people had dug up for him which contained a supply of various liquors; air conditioning; a coffee percolator, which plugged into an outlet by his dressing-table mirror. All the comforts of home. Maxvil learned from Lou Nason, the stage manager, that this particular dressing room was normally used by several people, part of a chorus if the show were a musical, extras if it were a big production.

"Bob wanted space. People came and went. Since there were only five people in the cast of *Triangle* there was no reason not to give him the big room."

"You say people 'came and went,' " Maxvil said. "No check on people?"

"Oh, sure. Johnny Quill, the stage-door man. People had to pass him. I suppose, now and then, someone came in without Johnny seeing them—if he went to the john, or was running an errand for someone. But everything was real loose backstage here." Nason shook his head, remembering. "Bob Dale didn't have any star complex. He loved people. Old ladies would come back to swoon over him after a matinee. He never shut anyone out. He had an army of friends who would drop in on him during the day or after a performance. The other actors had the run of the place. Bob Dale's dressing-room door was never locked."

"Ever hear anyone quarreling with him?" Maxvil asked.

"All the time I worked with him, which was only this show, I only heard him angry once," Nason said. "That was when the actor who was hired to play the wrestler turned up for rehearsal drunk. I say 'heard him,' but I almost didn't hear him, because he was so cold, so quiet.

When a guy controls his anger that way he's a little scarey. You knew Smallwood—that was the actor—could have pleaded with him till hell froze over and Bob wouldn't have changed his mind." Nason laughed. "I remember we were having a run-through during rehearsals. Jake Goldman, the guy who owns the theater, was out in the seats, talking to someone real loud. Jake always lets you know he's around. Bob stopped in the middle of a scene and spoke, very quietly, very precisely. 'I'm sorry, Jake,' he said, 'but the actors are making so much noise I can't hear what you're saying.' That shut the old bastard up. Of course Bob didn't have to back off from anyone. He was paying the rent on the house."

"I thought he and Hayes were producing *Triangle* together," Maxvil said.

"They were, but Bob put up the money. Gavin directed, handled the day-to-day business transactions, said yes or no to spending money for sets and props—and like that."

"But Dale and Hayes got along together?"

"They were different as day and night," Nason said. "Bob was open, warm, a happy man. Gavin was a sardonic, cold-blooded type, you know."

"I know."

"He was always cutting people down. Witty but deadly. But he and Bob had known each other so long, worked together so often, they understood each other. Gavin would throw some sly curve at Bob, and Bob would just laugh. He took direction from Gavin because he trusted his judgments as a director. But Bob would protect the other actors. I remember, early on, Gavin had been riding Eddie Marks, the juvenile, pretty hard. Bob took him aside in a break and said, 'You want a performance out of that boy, start acting like a human being for a change.' And Gavin changed his

188

approach. I guess he realized he'd gone too far with Eddie.''

Round and round and it always came up the same: Dale, the special good guy, Gavin, the snide man who could, however, be controlled by Dale. Each in his own way tops at what he did, personalities aside.

"They were a winning team," Nason said. "The one area where they were alike was in a demand for total professionalism by everyone in the company and crew. Dale got it by example. People who worked with him wanted to be as disciplined and precise as he was. Gavin got it with whips—but he got it. But it was that mutual goal, I think, that kept them together as a combination. The only time I ever heard Bob bad-mouth anyone was after he'd seen a play somewhere where an actor was playing games on stage, upstaging his fellow actors, playing tricks that gave him a scene that belonged to someone else. And not behind that actor's back, either. Baynard Parsons, a colossal ham who's starring in that comedy down the street, came backstage here one night, exuding stardom. There were quite a few people in Bob's dressing room. Bob gave Parsons a cold eye and said: 'This is a meeting place for professionals, Parsons. After watching you mess up your fellow actors in that little opera down the street I have to tell you you're not welcome here.' '' Nason laughed. "It was in somebody's column the next day. Parsons took to wearing black glasses on his way to the theater after that.''

"So he could make enemies," Maxvil said. "We know he made a violent one. Who, Mr. Nason?"

"You think I haven't asked myself that a thousand times since day before yesterday? Violent enough to clobber him to death? God Almighty. Would you believe, I went to see Parsons's performance after that encounter. We matineed on Wednesdays, he on Thursdays, so I could go. Parsons had stopped playing games and was giving a very solid performance. A couple of people in the show asked me to say thanks to Bob. Parsons may have hated Bob for a public rebuke, but he recognized it was justified. He stopped being a jerk."

The usual dead end. Parsons might be worth checking out, along with a thousand other people.

"No gossip, no hint of a violent quarrel or disagreement?" Maxvil asked, without hope.

"So help me, nothing, Lieutenant. We were a success. Successes breed good feelings. No cause for jealousy because no one else was ever considered for Bob Dale's part. Smallwood, whom you say can't be your man, was the only sour note in the whole thing."

"Thanks, anyway," Maxvil said.

"There's one thing, Lieutenant. Things that belonged to Bob; who gets them?"

"What kind of things?"

"Personal belongings. I forgot all about it, but a few days ago Bob gave me something to keep for him in the safe in my office."

"What was it?"

"It was a large manila envelope," Nason said. "I supposed it was a playscript. People were always bringing Bob scripts to read. I didn't look in the envelope. It was none of my business."

"Get it, will you?" Maxvil said. "Hell, we grab at any straws in this racket."

7

What goes on in a man's mind when he is going to kill someone against whom he has no grudge, who has done him no wrong, for whom he feels a genuine respect? That man's ego must be staggering, Peter thought. He was facing death for the simple reason that Max Lewis didn't "intend to be caught."

Lewis had come here because he hadn't found his play-script among Sam Cowley's things. By coming here he would certainly reveal to Peter that he was the killer, and therefore Peter would have to be eliminated. That script was more important than another human life, and perhaps another and another. Lewis was going to get it back no matter what the cost.

The gun in Lewis's hand didn't waver by a hair. The man had extraordinary muscular control. Nothing in his slightly contorted face suggested that he was debating any kind of choice, considering any kind of alternative. It was just a question of whether it would be now, or a minute from now, or five minutes from now. Peter knew that if he made one quick, desperate move toward Lewis, that would be that.

Seem interested in their problem whatever it is, ask about it, sympathize with it.

"It's hard to imagine what Dale and Hayes can have done to you, Max, to drive you to murder," Peter said. "You are a sophisticated man, a man of tastes in the arts. Murder doesn't fit you as I read you at all. As a critic you had a certain power over them, yet you gave their production a dazzling notice that guaranteed its success."

"I never let personal feelings compromise my honesty as a critic," Lewis said.

"I believe that. For years you have been my guide to good plays on Broadway. I've been to plays you didn't like, too, and I've never felt you were unfair in what you said about them. Perhaps a little cruel in the *way* you said it, but honest. What did they do to you, Max, or threaten to do?"

"Put an end to my career," Lewis said, dangerously quiet. "Destroying my standing as a critic. Cost me everything that matters to me, my way of life, my prestige in the theater and among theater people. That's all that has ever mattered to me, Peter."

"And murder won't wreck all that?"

"It won't," Lewis said, that thin slit of a smile tightening, "because I won't be caught. No one would dream that Max Lewis, man about town, gifted critic, literary sophisticate, could kill. You didn't dream it, did you, Peter?"

"No."

"But you know now, and I can't let you destroy me. I'm sorry. I'm really very sorry."

Peter caught in his breath. He thought it would be right then. "I don't understand why you came here, Max. I don't understand why you revealed yourself to me."

"Because you know!" Lewis said, his voice rising.

Easy, for Christ sake! *Sympathize!*

"But I don't know, Max," Peter said urgently. "I don't know what you think I know."

"The Wallace girl. She must have told you. You spent hours with her."

"She didn't tell me anything. I don't remember that your name was ever mentioned in the time I spent with her."

"Dale had to have told her," Lewis said. "Sooner or later she will remember. I think she must certainly have passed it on to you. Maybe you haven't connected it yet with what's happened. But you will—or would have. And she will, unless I get to her."

"Max, I swear to you there was nothing. She doesn't know anything about you. Oh, she may have mentioned your good review in *Newsview*, but nothing else."

Uncertainty clouded the killer's eyes. "She was in the hay with Dale every night. She was more than just a one-night stand with him. they were close, intimate. He would have told her something that gave him pleasure. And what the sonofabitch had on me gave him pleasure. He was waiting for just the right moment to give me the business."

"But he hadn't?"

"Because I stopped him. And I stopped Hayes with whom he'd shared what he had. But then—then I couldn't find it."

"Your play?"

"Yes. I told you he might have made notes, but not the kind of notes you thought I meant."

"What is there about the play, Max? You must have been satisfied with it or you wouldn't have given it to Dale to read."

"It's a good play. It's a first-rate play. It's a damned good play!" Lewis said, voice rising with each sentence.

"Surely you have copies of it," Peter said. "It isn't lost

just because you can't find the copy you gave Dale."

"Oh, I have copies of it," Lewis said. "My agent has a copy of it, a couple of producers have copies of it. They're actually trying to outbid each other for the right to produce it. A hit play by Max Lewis would be a winner. The great hatchet man has the courage to stick out his own neck, face the firing squad of which he has always been a member. And a triumph!" For the first time the gun seemed to shake slightly in his hand. "It would have been the greatest moment of my life."

"Still could be, Max. Still will be if you can get away with murder."

"Damn you, Peter, did Deborah tell you where the script is?"

"She never mentioned it to me."

"Sam Cowley said he had something. Had *something*? Did he mention the script to you?"

"No. Max, what is it? You've written a good play. People are beating on your door to produce it. And you set out on a murder rampage. Before you pull that trigger you just have to tell me what it is. What did Dale and Hayes have on you?"

"They knew I didn't write the play, goddamn them!" Lewis shouted. "They were waiting for someone to announce it, and then they would blow me to hell and gone. Dale had such a fetish about professional honesty in the theater. Hayes saw it as a way to hang me by my thumbs, and a successful cruelty was champagne and caviar to him."

"You didn't write the play, Max?"

"It was the wildest kind of coincidence," Lewis said. "Three years ago I was in Hollywood for the Academy Awards. Couple of Broadway people were up for Oscars. A young playwright came to me with the script of a play and asked if I'd read it. That's not unusual. Max Lewis, the great critic, is often asked to read scripts." His bitterness was almost a wail of pain. "I told this young man—named Richard Larsen—that I couldn't get to it until after I'd returned to New York. He was grateful for anything. Don't get ideas, Peter." The gun steadied.

"Well, I got back here and the next day I read that Richard Larsen had been killed in a car crash out on the Coast. Tough for him. I dug out his script and read it. It was so good I couldn't believe it. It was just the kind of play I might have written—if I could write a play!

"I didn't think of anything then, but I didn't know where to send the script. I expected to hear an announcement any day. Any agent who had it would have found a producer without any trouble. But there was never any announcement, never anything more about Richard Larsen. Two years went by and I began to get the idea. I added a few Max Lewis touches to the script and offered it as my own. Why not? Larsen was gone.

"The leading part in the play would have fitted Bob Dale like a glove. If I had him to offer along with the play, I had a gold mine. And so, I gave him a copy to read.

"He sent for me four days ago, and I came here to your apartment to see him. We sat down, and he took my script and another script out of a manila envelope.

" 'You thieving sonofabitch,' he said. 'This is Dick Larsen's play, not yours. I've had this script ever since just before he died. I've been waiting for the right moment to do something about it.'

"It seemed Larsen had been an extra in some film Dale had made. Dale became a friend. He was friendly with everyone. Larsen gave him a script at the same time he gave one to me. A couple of days later Larsen was dead. Larsen left a wife out on the Coast, it seems. Dale had optioned the play from her and provided her with eating money till he was ready to do something with it.

" 'You try to do anything with this, Max,' he told me, 'and you won't live to talk about it.'

"Then he told me not to come here looking for the script, he'd have it stashed away somewhere. I suspected he'd have confided in Hayes, who would have been delighted to do me in—just for the pleasure of it. So, that night I came back here and killed him."

Peter stood very still. The gun was moving slightly, rising so that it was aimed straight at his face.

"I figured I was done for, but accounts squared. Hayes would talk to the cops. But he didn't! I think I know why. He wanted the pleasure of doing me in himself. So I went to the Boswell Theater the next night and waited for him. When he saw me in the doorway of his office he laughed. 'Stolen any new ideas lately?' he asked. And I shot him right between the eyes."

"And the girl had to be next, because she might know?" Peter asked. His throat was dry, his tongue felt thick. He could see death in the twisted face just a few feet away.

"And then you, Peter, because she would surely remember and tell you. And Sam Cowley; he was the kind of man Dale might have confided in, might have given the scripts to compare. Do you suppose the old jerk only had some more gossipy dirt to dish out to you?"

"I think he could never have kept the real story to himself for five minutes," Peter said. "If he knew, you can bank on it he's told someone, Max. So there's no point in this, is there? The scripts will turn up. Someone will figure it out."

"I'm sorry, Peter," Lewis said, his voice trembling now.

"I have to take the chance—and I can't take it with you. There is no way you could be persuaded to keep it buried. I know that. And so—"

There was the sound of breaking glass behind Peter, and Max Lewis's face exploded as though there had been a bomb in his head. He toppled over, his gun going off in a last convulsive effort, the shot going way wide of Peter. Peter found himself down on his hands and knees, retching.

Someone touched his shoulder, gently.

"Take it easy, man," Lieutenant Maxvil said. "It's all over."

It may be true that a drowning man's life passes before his eyes before he goes down for the third time. Peter Styles had been closer to death than any drowning man floundering to stay afloat, a split second away from dying, and there had been no replay of his life. All he had been thinking of was how to delay the end, how to divert Lewis's attention for the moment that would give him a chance to live. He had been concerned with survival and only survival.

Maxvil had led Peter out into the sunlit garden and eased him down into a wicker armchair. The apartment was swarming with Homicide people for the second time in three days. Peter sat with eyes shut, trying to suck in the sunlight through every pore of his body. The sunlight was life, helping to wipe out that terrible vision of Max Lewis's face dissolving in front of him.

"Police department sharpshooter," Maxvil said. He was standing by the chair, his hand still reassuringly on Peter's shoulder. "He was in that second-floor window just across the alley. You owe him a drink one of these days. We didn't dare try to break in. We figured you were in the hands of a lunatic, hopefully stalling him. From across the way we could see him holding a gun on you. My orders to the sharpshooter were that as soon as he could get Lewis in his sights—without a piece of you—he was to squeeze it off, let him have it.''

"But how did you know I was here with him?" Peter asked. His voiced sounded far away to him, like a stranger's.

"Bits and pieces," Maxvil said. "And luck. Bob Dale's lawyer showed up. His last contact with Dale had been a phone call in which Dale asked about the laws on plagiarism. That didn't mean anything to me. I didn't hook it up. You know me, pal, the bright young genius at Homicide. Later I went to the theater to talk to the stage manager, Lou Nason. Round and round the mulberry bush. Nothing. But as I was leaving he turned over a manila envelope to me, something Dale had given him for safekeeping. Nason thought it might be a playscript someone had given Dale to read. Dale was given dozens of scripts to read by bright young hopefuls. I didn't even bother to look at it. You know me, the Homicide genius! But I turned it over to Wilfred Joyce at headquarters—my bright young man with the wooden blocks? He was back to me in five minutes. There were two plays in the envelope, identical except for the title page. One title page indicated the play was written by Max Lewis, the other by Richard Larsen." Maxvil indulged in a short, grim little laugh. "Some of the fog began to dissolve in my brain. The lawyer had mentioned plagiarism. This could be it. Max Lewis! He could have been in the newsroom at the magazine, overheard my call to Devery about bringing the Wallace girl there. Nobody would have paid any particular attention to him—he had a right to be there, like the furniture. He knew the Newsview Building like his own home. Could be, I told myself. Could be.

"Meanwhile Deborah Wallace kept pestering me about you. Maybe you owe her a drink too. What was taking you so long? Why hadn't you come back when you said you would? To get her off my back I phoned Sergeant Danvers at The Players. Were you there? He told me you'd left the club an hour ago to head for your apartment, pick up clothes, and return uptown. I tried to call you, but there was no answer."

"I was here," Peter said, "with a psycho pointing a gun at my heart."

Maxvil nodded. "Where the Maxvil genius began to work," he said. "You'd told Lewis in my presence and Devery's about the call from Sam Cowley. You'd suggested that Cowley might be his best source for the piece he was allegedly writing on Dale. If Lewis was our psycho, you could be in big trouble. We got access to the apartment across the alley. That's another drink you owe, the guy who let us use his place without a warrant. He also had a pair of binoculars—opera glasses, he called them. I took a look, and through the glass of the French doors to this garden I saw you both, him holding a gun on you, you talking for your life, I guessed. He was facing those French doors. If I came over the fence, he'd see me. If we tried smashing in the front door, you'd be dead before we got into the room. Would you believe I waited there for fifteen minutes for my sharpshooter to show up. I was praying for you, pal. I was praying that your gift of gab would hold out."

"I guess I was praying, too—in a way," Peter said.

"It was a far-out chance," Maxvil said. "But it worked."

Peter breathed in the warm fresh air. "You think Sam Cowley knew about the plagiarism, had seen the two plays that were really one play?"

"It's just possible we won't ever know for sure," Maxvil said. "If Dale gave him the plays to look at, he took them

199

back later and turned them over to Nason for safekeeping."

"Why did Dale delay doing anything?" Peter asked. "Why did he give Max Lewis time to get at him?"

"The laws on plagiarism," Maxvil said. "There really isn't any law against Lewis's having a copy of the play typed up with his own name on it instead of the real author's. Only if he took money for it. Only if there was publicity on it that claimed the play was his. I understand that was close—two producers bidding for it. Dale was waiting for that to happen so he could nail Lewis legally. He didn't realize he was inviting his own murder, and the murder of his partner, Gavin Hayes, in whom he'd confided."

"And Sam Cowley?"

Maxvil shrugged. "My guess is yes. But I wonder if Dale would have shown him the plays, knowing that gossip was a disease with him? On the other hand the old boy probably knew all there was to know on the subject of plagiarism. Young playwrights have been stealing from him for years."

"I think that pleased him," Peter said. "The Old Master." He looked at his friend. "He wouldn't talk to you because there were 'judgments' to be made. What judgments, do you suppose?"

"Who knows? If he'd seen the plays and knew what Dale had known, he might have felt there was a 'judgment' to make. He might have felt that nailing Lewis for a literary theft was more important than nailing him for a murder. First things first. Literary honesty, professional integrity, had been the old man's life."

"And Dale never mentioned any of this to Deborah?"

"She says not. I haven't had time to talk to her myself, but Sergeant Croft says she never heard Dale mention a play by Max Lewis, or that it was not really his." Maxvil shook his head. "To kill four men just to save his reputation! It's hard to absorb."

"I don't know, Greg," Peter said. "What possession does a man have more valuable than that—his reputation? After all, what do I have but my reputation as an investigative reporter? What do you have but your reputation as the genius of the Homicide Division?"

They looked at each other. It was a relief to be able to laugh.